M.C. Beaton is the author of the hugely successful Agatha Raisin, Hamish Macbeth and Edwardian murder mystery series, all published by Constable & Robinson. She left a full-time career in journalism to turn to writing, and now divides her time between the Cotswolds, Paris and Istanbul.

Penelope Goes To Portsmouth

Being the Third Volume of the Travelling Matchmaker

M. C. BEATON

ROBINSON

Constable & Robinson Ltd
3 The Lanchesters
162 Fulham Palace Road
London W6 9ER
www.constablerobinson.com

First published in the US by St Martin's Press, 1991

First published in the UK by Robinson,
an imprint of Constable & Robinson Ltd, 2011

A copy of the British Library Cataloguing in
Publication data is available from the British Library

ISBN: 978-1-84901-481-6

Typeset by TW Typesetting, Plymouth, Devon

Printed and bound in the EU

3 5 7 9 10 8 6 4 2

1

*. . . an indolent, thoughtless, innocent sort of man that
will be continually in scrapes, and that will not get
forward with all his extraordinary talents, unless
somebody take him up and push him on . . .*

Creevey Papers

Miss Pym awoke with a start and wondered for a
moment where she was. She drew aside the bed
hangings. The dull-red glow of a dying fire on the
hearth revealed an inn bedchamber. But which inn?
she wondered blearily. She seemed to have been in so
many since she started her travels.

Then memory came flooding back. Of course! She
was in a bedchamber in the White Bear in Piccadilly
and shortly to set out on the road to Portsmouth.

Miss Pym had no business to take her to Portsmouth, no relative, only a desire to travel and, above
all, to look upon the sea for the first time. She had

already made two exciting journeys, one to Bath and one to Exeter. And what adventures she had had! Her life spent as a servant in the household of Mr Clarence seemed far away. And yet only a short time ago, she had been housekeeper at Thornton Hall in Kensington, looking forward to a bleak life of servitude. Then Mr Clarence had died and left her a legacy.

Hannah Pym's thoughts turned to her late employer's brother, Sir George Clarence, Sir George who had shown her such friendship and who had promised to take her to the opera when she returned from Portsmouth, Sir George with his fine profile, blue eyes, and silver hair.

She rose from her bed and drew off a pair of white cotton gloves, for she slept with her hands covered in goose grease and lemon juice in an attempt to soften and whiten them; although they were well-shaped, they were still a trifle red and coarse.

She was a thin, spare woman in her forties with square shoulders and slender hands and feet. She had thick sandy hair and odd-coloured eyes, like opals, which changed colour according to her mood. Her face was sallow, her mouth long and humorous, and her nose crooked. Her crooked nose and her sandy hair were the bane of her life. Had Sir George not already seen her sandy hair, she would have dyed it brown or some other fashionable colour. She gave a characteristic pull at her nose, fell to her knees and prayed to God to send her humility so that she might not long to wake up one morning and find her hair brown and her nose straight.

Her prayers over, she opened her trunk and took out a fine travelling-gown of brown velvet, for it was now March and the weather was still blustery and cold. Hannah had a good stock of expensive gowns and cloaks and hats. Urged by Sir George, she had taken her late employer's wife's wardrobe as her own, for pretty Mrs Clarence had run away with a footman so very long ago and had not taken anything with her. As she dressed, Hannah thought about Mrs Clarence and wondered what had become of her. Did she know her husband was dead and that she was free to marry her footman? Hannah could never blame her for having run away. Mrs Clarence had been so bright and kind and witty and Mr Clarence so moody and dark and depressing. He had shut up half the house after his wife had run away, and no longer entertained. Hannah had considered him heart-broken, but after his brother told her that Mr Clarence had always been moody and depressed, Hannah had come to the conclusion that he would have degenerated into a semi-recluse whether his wife stayed or went.

There was a tremendous bustle and noise in the inn, but then there always was in coaching inns, which turned night into day with the constant coming and going of travellers.

Hannah rang the bell and commanded the waiter to carry down her trunk to the stage. She tipped him and then followed him down the corridor, avoiding the outstretched hands of the other servants who congregated outside inn rooms like gannets as soon as a guest left. Disappointed, they told Hannah what

3

they thought of her, but Hannah turned a deaf ear to their complaints. She had arrived late the night before, had not dined, and had no reason to tip anyone. The towels in her room had not been clean but had simply been put in the linen press and had been still dirty from use by previous owners. The room itself had been dirty but at least free of bugs, unlike the City coaching inns, where bugs were a plague. Describing a stay at the Belle Savage on Ludgate Hill, Parson Woodforde, that famous diarist wrote, 'I was bit so terribly with buggs again this night that I got up at four o'clock in the morning and took a long walk by myself about the City till breakfast time.' The following night, he said, 'I did not pull off my cloathes . . . but sat up in a Great Chair all night with my Feet on the bed and slept very well considering and not pestered with buggs . . .'

Outside in the courtyard stood the coach, the Portsmouth Flyer. It was the usual Flying Machine, as the stage-coaches were called, high and covered in black leather and with red leather curtains at the oval windows. Hannah was curious to meet her travelling companions.

She was the first to board the coach and so she took her favourite seat in the left-hand corner, facing the horses. The day was windy and cold, and high above the courtyard, great angry clouds were racing each other across the sky, giving the impression that the moon was tearing across the heavens at such speed that one felt the night should be over in a twinkling.

The carriage bobbed and lurched as an outside passenger climbed on the roof. Then another. But where were the insiders? At ten minutes to six – ten minutes before the hour of departure – the carriage door opened and a fussily dressed lady climbed in. She was wearing a huge bonnet like a coal-scuttle out of which a sharp angry little face peered, rather like some vole-like creature staring out of a hole on the river-bank. The eyes rested on Hannah, a sniff emerged from the coal-scuttle, and the woman sat down with a bump.

'Cold morning,' remarked Hannah pleasantly. The woman sniffed again but did not reply.

For a moment, Hannah forgot that coach passengers usually avoided speaking to each other and the old servant in her felt cowed, imagining that the woman had sensed her low origins. Then Hannah gave her nose a defiant pull. She was now Miss Hannah Pym, gentlewoman, and on her return from Portsmouth, Sir George Clarence would take her to the opera. The carriage door opened again and a drab-looking middle-aged man climbed in. He had a bad cold and sniffed loudly. The coal-scuttle sniffed in disapproval. The man sniffed again. The coal-scuttle sniffed louder. Hannah giggled and both glared at her.

'I am sorry my cold amuses you,' said the man. He had a red face that looked as if it had been recently boiled. He had mutton-chop whiskers of fiery red and red-veined eyes.

'Forgive me,' said Hannah. 'I had just remembered

something vastly amusing. I am monstrous sorry for you, sir. Allow me to introduce myself. I am Miss Pym of Kensington.'

'Mr Jonas Cato of Fairfax,' said the man. 'Fact is I feel devilish poor.'

'I should not be travelling on the common stage,' said the coal-scuttle. 'I am Miss Abigail Trenton and my carriage had gone ahead with my luggage. I hope I may not catch your cold, Mr Cato, for I am a delicate creature and my chest is weak.'

'Sorry, ma'am, but I must get to Portsmouth to catch my ship.'

'Are you in the navy, Mr Cato?' asked Hannah.

'No, Miss Pym. Overseer on a tobacco plantation in Virgina.'

'An *American*!' Miss Trenton sounded as appalled as if he had confessed to being a primitive savage. 'That explains it.'

'Explains what?' demanded Mr Cato sharply.

'Your disregard of the health of your fellow passengers,' said Miss Trenton. 'Americans are famous for the crudity of their manners.'

'I ain't met a one that could beat bad manners when it comes to the likes of you,' said Mr Cato. 'And that business of your carriage going on ahead is all a hum if you ask me. Every coach in this country seems to contain a lady who swears she's really got her own carriage and it's gone on ahead. All we need now is a drunken sailor and you will have the usual passenger list of an English coach.'

'How dare you, sir!' cried Miss Trenton. 'I do so

have my own carriage and . . . and . . . it is green and well-sprung and with my John on the box and . . .'

'Now, now,' said Hannah soothingly in the voice that had quelled more than one squabble in the kitchens of Thornton Hall, 'if we are to travel together to Portsmouth, let us not fight and argue.'

Miss Trenton did not reply but took out a small book and began to read it. Mr Cato blew his nose mournfully, winked at Hannah, crossed his arms on his chest and closed his eyes.

The carriage door on Hannah's side opened, letting in a blast of cold air. There were several elegant men outside carrying a limp body. 'In he goes,' they cried.

An elegant young man was thrust into the coach and placed in the corner opposite Hannah. She realized he was dead drunk. His pallor was alarming and he was completely unconscious but he reeked of spirits and stale tobacco. One of the young men who had arranged him in the corner turned and smiled at Hannah as he climbed down from the coach. 'Been drinking deep, has our Gus. Watch he don't cascade on your shoes, ma'am.' Then he slammed the door.

Hannah eyed the young man nervously and drew her feet as far under the seat as they would go lest the young man did decide to be sick. She studied his face in the light of the carriage lamp.

He was very beautiful. He had a perfect profile and alabaster skin. Ridiculously long black silky eyelashes were fanned out over his cheeks. His mouth was a perfect piece of sculpture and his guinea-gold hair was in tumbled curls under his hat. His long legs were muscular and strong. His clothes were of the finest, and he had sixteen strings to his breeches.

Mr Cato opened his eyes and squinted sideways at the sleeping gentleman. 'There you are,' he said. 'The ruin of England. Drink and laziness. Dead before he's thirty.' Then Mr Cato closed his eyes again.

Hannah opened her reticule and brought out a small flask of rose-water and sprinkled some on the carriage floor to counteract the smell of stale spirits emanating from the young man.

Up on the roof, the guard blew a blast on the yard of tin. The young man stirred and groaned and opened his eyes. Like the rest of him, his eyes were beautiful; they were deep sapphire-blue. They rested on Hannah and winced.

'The deuce,' said the young man faintly. 'Where am I?'

'On the Portsmouth Flying Machine,' replied Hannah.

'That's all right then,' he said sleepily.

'You are not, sir,' said Hannah sharply, 'going to be sick?'

He looked at her vaguely. 'I cannot promise I won't.'

'Then will you please try to be sick *outside* the carriage!'

'Do my best, ma'am. What's that awful smell?'

'You, sir.'

'Faugh. Change and bathe at the next stage. Oh, God in Heaven and all His angels protect me!' This cry of pain was because the coach had struck a hole in the road. The young gentleman clutched his fair curls and groaned.

Hannah's eyes were by now fairly snapping with curiosity. She noticed the fine sapphire in his cravat, the splendour of his boots, the fineness of his linen. Here surely was an aristocrat, and an aristocrat on the stage was a mystery and mystery meant adventure.

He looked about to fall asleep again, so Hannah spoke up. 'We have all introduced ourselves. I am Miss Hannah Pym of Kensington. The other lady is Miss Abigail Trenton, and the gentleman, Mr Jonas Cato.'

'Railton, at your service, ma'am,' he said weakly.

'Mr Railton?' pursued Hannah.

'Lord Augustus Railton, if you must know,' he said.

Miss Trenton jerked upright, her mouth a little open. 'Oh, I am glad to make your lordship's acquaintance,' she gushed. 'So dreadful for us both to find ourselves in this stage, is it not? My carriage had gone ahead with my luggage. So much luggage, my lord, that there was no room for me. We shall no doubt catch up with it on the road.'

'And pigs may fly,' said Mr Cato.

Lord Railton or Lord Augustus? wondered Hannah. How should she address him? Then she remembered. Hannah read the social columns. Lord Augustus Railton was the younger son of the Earl of Tradmere. Therefore he should be addressed as Lord Augustus. What else had she heard of him? Surely there had been a trial in Bow Street? Something to do with breaking into the Duke of Duborough's house at midnight?

9

Hannah glanced out of the window. They would not cross the Thames until the coach reached Putney Bridge. She wished she had not been so thrifty and had eaten breakfast. But a bed at the White Bear was enough expense without adding meals on to it. Hannah had a small apartment above a baker's in the village of Kensington. It was too dangerous to travel from Kensington to London in a hack during the hours of darkness, and so she had decided to spend the night at the inn in Piccadilly. Would the road from Kensington ever be safe? Between Kensington and London lay Knightsbridge, the haunt of footpads and highwaymen. People wishing to walk from Kensington to Hyde Park Corner were meant to gather at the sound of a bell outside the entrance to Kensington Palace so that several could walk together in order to mitigate the perils of the journey.

Hannah looked rather sourly at Miss Trenton. Here she was with a real-life aristocrat and not a heroine in sight. There should have been a beautiful young lady in the carriage so that Lord Augustus could fall in love with her. Hannah was a determined matchmaker.

When Mrs Clarence had been in residence and Hannah had still only been a housemaid, there had been a young lady, a Miss Worthington, staying as a guest. A Mr Tamery had been much enamoured of this lady and she of him, but both were dreadfully shy and it looked to Hannah as if their visit to the Clarences might end with both of them going their separate ways without declaring their love.

And so she had declared it for them. She had

written a letter supposed to be from Mr Tamery to Miss Worthington, stating his passion and asking the lady to meet him in the gardens. How frightened the young Hannah had been at her own temerity. How amazed she had been later, as she had learned to spell and write better, that her scheme had worked so well. For both had promptly become engaged, Mr Tamery having been clever enough to keep quiet about not having written that ill-spelt letter.

When Putney was reached, only Hannah was awake. She sent up a prayer for Mr Pitt, the Prime Minister, lying ill at Bowling Green House, and hoped he would recover soon. She wondered whether they would soon be at war again with France. Some newspapers said the Consul, Bonaparte, had fits of madness, and only his wife, the Creole, Madame Bonaparte, could tolerate him. Joséphine, Madame Bonaparte, was said to be vastly elegant. Hannah took comfort from that. Madame Bonaparte was forty. If a woman could be described as elegant at the age of forty, there was hope for such as Hannah Pym yet!

The coach crossed Putney Heath and then on to Kingston, where it rolled into the yard of the Castle.

Lord Augustus awoke with a groan. 'B'Gad. I've a stomach on me like a Bengal general,' he complained. Hannah drew her skirts close about her and eyed him nervously.

'Perhaps a breakfast will set you to rights, my lord,' she said. 'A few rashers of bacon . . .'

'Stop, I pray,' said Lord Augustus faintly. The carriage door swung open and the grog face of the coachman looked in. 'Breakfast, ladies and gents,' he said. 'And make it sharp.' He then held out his hand for tips.

Lord Augustus's pallor became tinged with a faint pink. He searched frantically in his pockets. It was customary for the gentlemen in a stage-coach to pay the ladies' tips and meals.

'I bet the food at this inn is rotten,' said Lord Augustus.

'Wager you it ain't,' said Mr Cato. 'Reputed to have the best fare on the Portsmouth road.'

Animation showed in his lordship's blue eyes. 'Five yellow boys says it ain't,' he said.

'Right,' agreed the American. 'But my decision, mind.'

Hannah could not help noticing the slight relief in Lord Augustus's eyes as Mr Cato tipped the coachman for all. They trooped into the inn, followed by the outside passengers who, like the outsiders they were, would have to wait until the insiders had been served.

The smell of frying bacon was so delicious and Hannah so hungry that she was sure Lord Augustus would lose his bet. Alas, cooking food usually smells more delicious than the reality. The stage-coach passengers sat down to a breakfast of greasy, smelly bacon, pock-marked bread that showed where the spots of mould had been cleverly cut from it, and evil coffee.

Mr Cato silently handed over five guineas, which Lord Augustus cheerfully pocketed. Milk laced with rum was offered all round but all waved it away, fearing that the milk was sour. Only Lord Augustus, who had ordered and drunk a large glass of brandy, looked cheerful when they mounted the coach again.

Miss Trenton poked her head out of the window and glared at the coachman, who was talking to the guard in the inn courtyard.

'Are we to be kept at this filthy place all day?' she shouted.

'Waiting another passenger,' said the coachman laconically.

'I shall give you five more minutes,' snapped Miss Trenton, 'and if we are not on our way by then, I shall report you to the owners!'

She slammed up the glass and peered around. 'Disgraceful!' she said. 'Of course, I suppose the blame must lie with this new passenger. People are so inconsiderate.'

'Be along soon enough,' drawled Lord Augustus. 'We'll be making another stop at Esher and might get something decent to eat there.' He smiled around lazily. 'Apologize for being bosky. Celebrating something, only can't remember what.'

'Perhaps this is our passenger arriving,' said Hannah, noticing a shabby post-chaise drawing up.

A young lady stepped down, followed by a stern matron. The carriage door was opened.

'In you go, Penelope,' said the matron. 'It is of no use trying to lie to your parents, for I have written them of your perfidy.'

The young lady murmured something unintelligible. Lord Augustus moved across the carriage to sit

13

next to Hannah and begged the young lady to take his seat at the window. She murmured her thanks. Her face was covered with a large handkerchief.

The carriage door slammed shut and the coachman and guard mounted to the roof.

Hannah took out a guidebook, prepared to read, but put it down again as she heard a soft exclamation of surprise from Lord Augustus. She put down her book and looked up.

The young lady had removed her handkerchief. Hannah stared at her, open-mouthed. Never had she seen such a vision of loveliness. The face of the young lady was heart-shaped. Under a frivolous little bonnet rioted dusky curls. Huge pansy-brown eyes stared out at the world in innocent wonder. She had a soft and generous mouth. Her lashes were long and tipped with gold. She was wearing a pink velvet gown with a pink velvet spencer. Two large tears welled up in her eyes and fell down her cheeks. Hannah thought the girl, for she was surely barely above seventeen years, had probably been crying for some time, although her cheeks were not blotched, nor were her beautiful eyes red.

Lord Augustus took out a large handkerchief and handed it to her. 'Thank you,' she said, and smiled, a bewitching smile. 'Mine is all wet. La! I have been crying this age.'

'What troubles you, my dear?' asked Hannah.

Penelope gave a little choked sob and then blew her button of a nose. It was an unfashionable nose, a pert little nose, a common nose, but it did not detract from

14

her beauty one whit. 'There,' she said in a soft voice. 'I shall cry no more. When people keep telling you and telling you that you are wicked, you begin to think it might be so. But I did not do anything wrong.'

'What did you do?' asked Hannah bluntly.

'I did not know his feelings were so warm towards me,' said Penelope earnestly. 'How could I? I mean, he was just the music teacher at the seminary and quite dreadfully old, nearly forty.' Hannah glared but Penelope went on regardless. 'He would put his hands over mine to show me the fingering of the keys, and say, "Naughty puss, you will never get it right," and then he would squeeze my fingers, but I thought it was a punishment. Then yesterday, Mr Turrip, the music teacher, that is, fell to his knees beside the piano stool and asked me to marry him. Imagine! And then Miss Jasper walked in.'

'Miss Jasper?' prompted Lord Augustus, his voice warm with amusement.

'The principal of the seminary. She said I had been leading him on and demanded to know all, after she had dismissed the poor man from her employ. I said I had not been leading him on and said he had squeezed my fingers as a punishment, and *she* said, no one in their right mind was as naïve as all that and that I had caused trouble before.'

'How had you caused trouble before?' Hannah leaned forward.

'It was in church, don't you see.' Penelope prattled on in a childlike voice. 'There was this young man kept staring at me and I thought perhaps I had a smut on my nose or perhaps he did not like me. So when we were filing out of the church – that is, I and the other girls – I stepped aside and demanded to know why he had looked at me so. He said his heart was breaking and I said that he would be better to stare at the lady who had broken his heart than glare at me, and Miss Jasper came up and gave my arm quite a cruel wrench and she said to the young man, "Your parents shall hear from me," so perhaps she knew why his heart was breaking. But I do not see why I was in disgrace.'

'Did it not perhaps occur to you that he was breaking his heart over *you*?' demanded Hannah.

Penelope's large eyes became even larger. 'No. Why should it? I mean, we had not been introduced.'

'Ah, I see you are a stickler for the conventions,' said Lord Augustus. He introduced himself and then the other members of the carriage. Hannah noticed in surprise that Lord Augustus had somehow managed to change his clothes, shave and wash during their brief stop at the Castle.

'And my name is Penelope Wilkins,' said the charmer. 'How d'ye do. I shall have your handkerchief laundered when I reach home, Mr Railton, and return it to you.'

'Lord Augustus Railton,' simpered Miss Trenton.

Penelope stared at Lord Augustus for a long moment. Then she said, 'If you are a lord, why are you on the common stage?'

'Pockets to let,' he remarked.

Penelope looked puzzled. 'Sported all my blunt,' he

volunteered by way of clarification. Penelope shook her head in bewilderment.

'He means he ain't got no money,' said Mr Cato and then let out a deafening sneeze.

'Oh.' Penelope digested this piece of information. 'But people do say, "As rich as a lord", do they not?'

'I think the phrase is, "As drunk as a lord",' said Hannah.

Another pouting 'oh' from that rosebud mouth. Then the pretty face cleared. 'Ah, that is why you do not have money. You lead a dissolute life.'

'My dear . . .' protested Hannah.

'Exactly,' said Lord Augustus.

'Then the situation can be remedied,' said Penelope. 'You can always work.'

Mr Cato slapped his knee in delight and chuckled. 'That's rich, that is. You sound like a Yankee,' by which he meant New Englander. 'Don't you know what a gentleman is, young lady? They don't work.'

'But my father works very hard,' said Penelope earnestly, 'and he is a gentleman.'

'What does he do?' asked Mr Cato curiously.

'He owns the biggest chandlery business in Portsmouth.' Penelope's eyes sparkled with pride.

'Then he's just like me,' said Mr Cato. 'You can't be a gentleman and be in trade.'

'That is not true,' said Penelope. 'Why, Mr Whitbread, the Member of Parliament, is in beer, and yet he dines with the Prince of Wales.'

'Ah, well, beer's another thing. Tea, too,' said Mr Cato darkly.

Penelope looked puzzled.

'You do not seem to know much of the world, Miss Wilkins,' said Hannah curiously. 'I gather you have been at a seminary in Kingston. Surely the purpose of such seminaries is to train young ladies in etiquette.'

'I suppose so,' said Penelope vaguely, 'and what a dead bore it was, too. Were I not in disgrace, I would be quite happy to go home. Papa is a dear but he has such ambitions for me. I had a governess at home and was not allowed to socialize with the daughters of the other tradespeople in Portsmouth. Papa says I am to marry a lord, but I do not think I want to, if they do not work.'

'But everyone in England falls out of their cradle knowing the aristocracy do not work,' said Mr Cato.

'Now that is not quite true,' said Hannah. 'Many do a great deal of work on their estates or in the army or the Church or in the government of the country. Pray tell Miss Wilkins you are not a good example.' Hannah gave Lord Augustus a quizzical look.

'You have the right of it, ma'am,' said Lord Augustus seriously. 'You have no idea the work we have, Miss Wilkins. It is a great deal of labour to be in fashion. Hours being fitted by one's tailor, lies to be thought up for the dun and one's banker, dancing with the most appalling females just to be polite, knowing who to cut and who to be civil to . . . faugh! I feel exhausted just thinking about it all.'

'What a dreadfully useless sort of life,' said Penelope mournfully.

'He is bamming,' said Hannah, looking hopefully at

18

Lord Augustus, waiting for that young man to redeem himself. But he cocked a quizzical eyebrow at her and said softly, 'Good try, ma'am, but it is as I say. I am beyond repair – just like my fortunes.'

But not, thought Miss Hannah Pym, if you marry a rich merchant's daughter.

2

Dumb, inscrutable and grand.

Matthew Arnold

The coach rolled to a stop at Esher. All were hungry, and when the coachman opened the door, Mr Cato, as spokesman, said they all needed a proper breakfast.

They filed into a low dining-room and clustered around the fire while the waiters rushed to set the table. Hannah looked curiously at Miss Trenton, wondering what she was like without her massive bonnet and then decided the lady would probably appear even more ill-favoured than she seemed with it on.

Miss Trenton seemed to have contracted a strong dislike for the fair Penelope.

This time the food proved excellent. Even Miss

Trenton showed signs of thaw, although she still concentrated mostly on Lord Augustus, regaling him with tales of her splendid carriage, which was always 'just up ahead'.

And then the cosy atmosphere was shattered. A man in irons was led through the dining-room and into the tap by two constables and three militia. He was dirty and dishevelled, a sorry figure indeed. He was tall and thin with thick smooth black hair and a clever mobile face with a beaky nose and long mouth, an East End London face, thought Hannah. His black eyes flashed a look of mute appeal at the assembled company. Miss Trenton and Mr Cato turned their faces away. Hannah looked back in curious sympathy, Penelope's eyes filled with tears, and Lord Augustus looked at Penelope and then shouted to one of the constables, 'What has he done?'

The constable turned back. 'Footman to Lady Carsey at the Manor. Robbed her of her diamond brooch, he did. Moving him to the prison here. He'll hang on the scaffold in the morning. Thirsty work, escorting prisoners.' He looked longingly at the rest, who were already burying their noses in pewter tankards in the tap.

Penelope let out a little squeal of dismay.

'I suppose the prisoner protests his innocence?' asked Lord Augustus.

'Can't. Deaf and dumb.'

Lord Augustus glanced at Penelope's wide-eyed distress, and said, 'And there is absolute proof he took it?'

'Well, her ladyship says so, and that was enough for the court.'

'But hanging,' protested Hannah. 'Surely transportation would be a more normal sentence for theft.'

'Not from a peeress, it ain't,' said the constable. 'If you're on the thieving lay, best to take from Mr Bloggs of nowhere and leave the quality alone.' And he walked off to join the others.

Penelope clenched her little hands. 'He is innocent,' she pronounced.

Miss Trenton found her voice. 'Do not be such a silly chit,' she said roundly. 'You have never seen the fellow before, and if Lady Carsey says he did it, then he did.'

'Are you acquainted with Lady Carsey?' asked Lord Augustus.

'No, but, well, it stands to reason . . .'

Penelope had begun to cry in earnest, and all looked at her helplessly.

Her food lay untouched in front of her. 'I do not understand your distress,' said Hannah, although she had to admit that that look from the prisoner had touched her heart. 'Excuse me.' She rose to her feet, and to the other passengers' surprise, she made her way through to the tap.

'I would like to speak to the prisoner,' she said.

'He can't speak, mum, nor hear,' said a constable.

Hannah looked into the prisoner's face. He seemed intelligent. She opened her reticule and drew out a notebook and a lead pencil. On a page she wrote, 'Did you take the brooch?'

22

She then passed both notebook and pencil to the prisoner. Holding them awkwardly, for his wrists were manacled, he leaned the book on top of the table and wrote, 'I am innocent.'

Hannah's eyes gleamed with excitement. 'Then why should she accuse you?' she wrote.

The prisoner read it and then began to write busily. 'She wanted me in her bed. I refused. She took this revenge. She probably still has the brooch.'

'Enough o' that,' growled the constable. 'Time to go.' Hannah took back her notebook and watched miserably as the prisoner was dragged out of the inn.

She read what he had written and then returned to the others. She silently showed the notebook to Penelope, who had to scrub her streaming eyes in order to read it.

'Oh, there you have it,' cried Penelope. 'He *is* innocent.' Her large and beautiful eyes turned on Lord Augustus. 'You must do something, my lord. You *can* do something.'

Lord Augustus took the notebook from her, read it, and shrugged his elegant shoulders. 'I cannot be of help,' he said indifferently. 'Deuced hot in here. Going outside for some air.'

Hannah slid an arm around Penelope's shaking shoulders. 'I do not think anyone can help now that the courts have passed a death sentence on him. All we can do is pray.'

Penelope clasped her hands and closed her eyes like an obedient child. Hannah felt a lump rising in her throat. Surely the man was guilty. He must be guilty.

The coachman called they were ready to leave and they all trudged out into the courtyard to where Lord Augustus was leaning against the side of the coach, smoking a cheroot.

They all climbed silently in. Even Mr Cato seemed to have been affected by the prisoner's fate. They were just leaving the courtyard when there came various splintering sounds. The carriage dipped suddenly, throwing everyone into a jumble of arms and legs.

Mr Cato was first to open the door. The front wheels of the coach had gone spinning away, the poles had snapped, and the cursing coachman was gingerly climbing down.

The coachman examined the damage and his face darkened with rage. 'Someone's taken a saw to these here poles and wheel shafts,' he shouted. 'Which one of you did this?'

The cold voice of Lord Augustus dripped like iced water on the rage of the coachman. 'My dear, dear fellow,' he said. 'You are surely not accusing one of us of sabotage.'

'Someone did it,' said the coachman, whirling this way and that.

'Then you had better summon the law,' remarked Lord Augustus equably, 'while I escort the ladies back to the inn.'

He held out one arm to Hannah and the other to Penelope. Miss Trenton muttered something and then walked behind them to the inn, followed by Mr Cato and the outside passengers.

'It is a miracle,' breathed Penelope.

'The coach breaking down?' Hannah began to wonder whether the fair Penelope had all her wits.

'Yes, you see, it gives us *time*.'

'Time for what?' demanded Hannah crossly.

'Why, time to visit Lady Carsey and ask her whether she is sure that the footman stole the brooch.'

'I do not see how a party of stage-coach passengers would be allowed further than her lodge-gates,' said Hannah.

Penelope's eyes rounded on Lord Augustus like carriage lamps turning a corner. 'But *you* could, my lord.'

'I am a Fribble, Miss Wilkins,' said Lord Augustus, leading her to the inn-table and drawing out a chair for her. 'A lily of the field. I toil not, neither do I interest myself in the fate of footmen.' He turned and walked stiffly from the inn. Penelope let out a cry of distress.

'Wait here with Mr Cato and Miss Trenton,' said Hannah. 'I shall be back in a trice.'

She found Lord Augustus standing in the coach-yard, studying the wreck of the coach through his quizzing-glass.

'If you took that saw out of your top-boot, my lord,' said Hannah quietly, 'then you might be able to join us and sit at your ease.'

He stood silently for a moment, and then gave a reluctant laugh. 'I hope no one else has such sharp eyes. I shall go round to the tack-room and replace it if you will make sure no one follows me.'

Hannah studied his retreating back thoughtfully. So the indolent Lord Augustus had moved himself enough to wreck the coach. Obviously he wanted to gain time to prove the footman's innocence or guilt to Penelope's satisfaction. Therefore, he must be interested in Penelope. He was obviously in need of funds and Penelope's father was rich. Penelope's father wanted his daughter to marry a lord. What could be more perfect? And Hannah was firmly convinced that behind the stiffening spine of every Fribble lay a pretty and spineless woman who needed protection. Hannah heaved a sigh. The meek shall inherit the best husbands. Women of character, brains, and independence were damned to spinsterhood unless they commanded a good dowry. Such was the way of the world.

Lord Augustus ambled back. 'Why did you do it?' asked Hannah.

'The food here is good,' he said carelessly, 'and I have a mind to stay the night in Esher.'

'But, my lord, surely you wish to prove the footman innocent?'

He laughed. 'Why, you are a romantic, Miss Pym, with a hellish gleam of matchmaking in your fine eyes. I have no interest in that soufflé of a young lady in there.'

'Do you mean to say,' said Hannah angrily, 'that you damaged the coach simply to prolong your stay here? I have a good mind to report you.'

'Don't,' he said lazily. 'They would bill me for the damage and my pockets are to let.'

'Then if you want to keep my mouth shut, sirrah, I

suggest you busy yourself with an immediate visit to Lady Carsey.'

'What a bully you are. Must I?'

'Of course!'

'So be it. But at least allow me a glass of brandy to fortify myself.'

Hannah sat impatiently in the inn while Lord Augustus sipped his brandy and looked vaguely about him. Penelope had retired upstairs to an inn bed-chamber to wash and change. 'I told her she was going to needless expense renting a room,' snapped Miss Trenton. 'Waste of time prettifying herself.'

'I do so agree,' said Lord Augustus earnestly. Miss Trenton beamed on him, but her smile faded when he added, 'Miss Wilkins is pretty enough as it is.'

Hannah rose to her feet. 'I am going out for a walk. I suggest you accompany me, Lord Augustus.' She gave him a threatening glare.

'Very well,' he said meekly.

'And you know just where we are going,' said Hannah, as they walked together across the inn courtyard. There was a quick patter of footsteps behind them and Penelope caught up with them. She was wearing a sapphire-blue carriage dress with gold frogs, and a frivolous little military hat was balanced rakishly on her dusky curls.

'I am coming with you,' she said.

'For a walk?' asked Lord Augustus.

'No, stoopid! To Lady Carsey.'

'Ladies, ladies, may I point out we do not know where she lives.'

'But I do,' said Penelope triumphantly. 'She lives at the Manor. The constable said so, and the Manor is only a short walk from here. I asked the servants. We turn to the left.'

A blustery wind whipped at the ladies' skirts. Penelope stifled a yawn. 'I am so very tired.' She smiled up at Lord Augustus. 'Of course, as soon as we set our footman free, I can catch a few hours' sleep.'

'You are so confident,' he said.

A dazzling smile met his gaze. 'Oh, but you see, I have quite decided you could do anything at all, my lord, once you put your mind to it.'

'I am struck as dumb as the footman,' remarked Lord Augustus.

'What takes you to Portsmouth, my lord?' asked Hannah.

'I have an aged uncle in residence there. Quite rich. Bound to die soon. My last hope. Now what have I said?' For Penelope's face was puckered up in distress.

'You are like a vulture, my lord, waiting for that old man to die. Fie, for shame!'

A glint of anger showed in Lord Augustus's blue eyes. Beautiful widgeons such as Penelope were supposed to make pretty, artless remarks. Then he smiled. 'I feel I am reliving my grandfather's experiences.'

'How so? A story?' Penelope clasped both hands over his arm and looked at him as hopefully as a child at bed-time.

'A true story, Miss Wilkins. My father, when a very young man, was taken prisoner by the Americans in 1777 and put on board a prison ship above Charlestown Ferry in Boston. The ship was foul and he and his fellow officers were suffering from fever, ague, and dysentery. They wrote to the Council of Boston and asked leave to go into the country on parole. This was granted and he was told his parole would be in the town of Pepperell, although he would not be allowed to travel over a mile outside the town. He procured quarters for himself and his servant in a house where he had to pay two silver dollars a week for board.

'It was a free and easy existence. The family consisted of a middle-aged couple and their two spinster daughters. They had not the least understanding of what was due to a gentleman and treated my father's servant in exactly the same way as they treated my father. My father said he quite enjoyed the evenings when a large fire would be made on the hearth. The room was filled with the sound of humming spinning-wheels and the laughter of the apprentice boys shucking corn. No candles were used, but the room was lighted by splinters of pine wood thrown on the fire. The days were boring, he said; nothing to do while the family were out at work. And when he asked the town council for washerwomen to do his laundry, they sent him a wash-tub and a bar of soap and told him to get on with it. You should live in America, Miss Wilkins.'

There was a silence. Penelope frowned in thought. 'You are mocking me,' she said at last. 'But if he was a prisoner, washing his own clothes was surely not such a hardship.'

'My dear young lady, the joke is that they should expect him to do so.'

'Why?'

'Gentlemen do not wash their own clothes.'

'How very strange to stand on ceremony in such circumstances,' said Penelope thoughtfully. 'Stupid, too. And had he and his servant volunteered to help the family in their work, they would not have found the days boring.'

'Have you ever done any work yourself, Miss Wilkins?'

'No. But then I have not been a prisoner of war, but if I ever were, I should not stand on my dignity.'

'Easy to say when it is not likely to happen.'

The couple surveyed each other coldly, as if across a great gulf.

Hannah stifled a sigh. Despite Père Wilkins's worldly ambitions for his daughter, she feared he was a Radical, and would not look fondly on such as the frivolous Lord Augustus as a son-in-law. Like most people at the dawn of this new nineteenth century, Hannah believed that God put one in one's appointed place and to think otherwise was flying in the face of Providence. In her case, it was different. Divine Intervention had seen to it that she was left a legacy. And yet there was no denying the common sense of Penelope's argument. Perhaps Penelope was not stupid at all, but merely unfashionably down-to-earth.

They came to the gates of the Manor. Lord Augustus rang the bell at the lodge and then presented his card to the lodge-keeper, who opened the gates.

They walked in silence up to the house. Again Lord Augustus presented his card. A butler led them through a shadowy hall to a reception room and then left them. The house appeared to be richly furnished, but somehow cold and dark and gloomy.

They waited half an hour and then the door opened and Lady Carsey came in.

Penelope took one look at her, turned pink, and stared at the floor. For despite the chilly day, Lady Carsey was wearing a transparent muslin gown and appeared to have next to nothing under it. She was highly painted, Roman-looking, with a generous bust, liquid eyes, a patrician nose, and a great quantity of glossy brown curls dressed in the latest fashion. She held out her hand to Lord Augustus and then gave two fingers for Penelope and Hannah to shake. Hannah wondered crossly why Lady Carsey had immediately assumed that she and Miss Wilkins were of lower rank than Lord Augustus. Covertly, Hannah stroked the expensive stuff of her gown. Why had not Lady Carsey thought them relatives?

But Lady Carsey knew all about the stage-coach passengers, having just heard the gossip about them from her servants. She had learned all about the handsome lord and the 'divinely beautiful' girl who had arrived on the stage, and so it was Penelope she was trying to offend, not Hannah.

She waved a hand to indicate that they had her permission to sit down, and then asked Lord Augustus, 'And to what do I owe the pleasure of this visit?'

'The ladies here have had their hearts touched by

the predicament of your footman,' said Lord Augustus. Lady Carsey's eyes, which had been glowing at
him a moment before, hardened. 'He is a thief. He
stole my brooch.'

'Why did you employ a deaf-and-dumb footman in
the first place?' asked Lord Augustus curiously.

She shrugged. 'A novelty. It amused me to have a
dumb servant. Now, if I have satisfied your curiosity,
you must excuse me. I have much to do.'

'I see we have bored you with our tedious inquiries,' said Lord Augustus. 'Perhaps I can redeem
myself by giving you the latest London gossip.' He
smiled into her eyes.

'Perhaps. But have these ladies nothing else to do?'

'Of course,' said Lord Augustus. 'They are both
fatigued and would be glad of an opportunity to rest.
Is that not so, Miss Pym?'

Hannah got to her feet. 'Certainly. Come, Miss
Wilkins.'

Penelope's eyes were wide with disappointment as
Hannah urged her from the room. 'He was not
interested in helping our footman,' expostulated
Penelope. 'He is only interested in that painted harridan.'

'Then he has more chance of finding out whether
the footman really took the brooch or not than we
have,' said Hannah crossly. She hoped that was what
Lord Augustus meant to do, but she doubted it. She
wondered if Lord Augustus had ever thought seriously about anyone or anything in the whole of his life.

'We can go and see our prisoner, however,' said
Hannah, 'and take him some food.'

Penelope brightened. Then her face fell. 'But we cannot offer him any hope, and with the prospect of the gallows before him, he may not feel like eating anything.'

They returned to the inn and found out the whereabouts of the prison, packed a basket with eatables and a bottle of wine, and made their way out again. The day had turned cold and the sky was dark. Birds piped miserably in the bare branches of the trees. Outside the prison, they were erecting the gallows, the workmen whistling cheerfully.

Hannah had found out that the prisoner was called Benjamin Stubbs. She bribed the turnkey to obtain permission to talk to the prisoner for half an hour.

They were shown into a miserable cell. Benjamin was chained to the floor. Penelope gave a childish little gulp and Hannah knew the girl was trying hard not to cry. She held out a piece of paper on which she had already written: 'We have brought you some food.'

The prisoner gave her a wan smile and it went straight to Hannah's heart. The footman had a face that Hannah was sure was normally bright and cheeky and alert. She took out another piece of paper and wrote, 'How did you come to be in Lady Carsey's employ?'

He sat down at a plain deal table in the cell and awkwardly took the paper and pencil from her, the long chains locked to the floor rattling and clanking as he moved.

He began to write busily while Hannah and Penelope sat in silence. At last he handed the paper over. Hannah and Penelope put their heads together and read, 'I had never been in Service and had a mind to be a Footman. I had been on the Rode for a Long Time, working in the Fields when I could. I had no References but heard Lady Carsey liked Freaks and had once taken a Dwarf in her employ as a page. Me being Deaf and Dumb might interest her and so it did, and so she hired me. But she wanted me in her Bed and I could not, for she was not to my Taste, and so she got Mad and said I had stole the Broach which I did not as sure as my name is Benjamin Stubbs.'

'Decadence,' said Hannah fiercely. She wrote, 'Describe the brooch.'

Again the prisoner wrote and again they read. 'It was an oblong brooch of Dymonds set in gold with little saffires around the Edge.'

Hannah wrote, 'Be of good cheer. We will do what we can to help.'

Tears formed in the prisoner's eyes and he turned his head away.

'How terrible,' sobbed Penelope when they were once more outside the prison. 'B-but how odd that Lady Carsey should collect freaks.'

'Painted harpy,' said Hannah with a sniff. 'If such is to Lord Augustus's taste, I want nothing more to do with him.'

When they returned to the inn, it was to learn that the stage-coach would be repaired the following morning. There was no sign of Lord Augustus. The day wore on and then he appeared. He requested a bedchamber, went upstairs, and came down a half-hour later, very grand in evening dress, cool and tailored and barbered. Hannah asked him eagerly if there was any hope of finding the brooch, but he looked at her vaguely and said he was going to the Manor for dinner. Still hopeful, Hannah gave him a description of the brooch. He did not appear to pay any great attention. He had become haughty and remote. Even Miss Trenton voiced as soon as he had gone that she was disappointed in such a man who did not know the proper respect due to a lady such as herself who owned a carriage.

After dinner, Mr Cato and Miss Trenton retired to the bedchambers they had been forced to reserve, neither wanting to sit up all night. But Hannah and Penelope sat on in the dining-room, looking from time to time out of the bay window, hoping for a glimpse of Lord Augustus coming back with some good news. Neither of the ladies really could believe that the indolent Lord Augustus would make an effort to do anything.

Midnight came and went. 'You should get some sleep, Miss Wilkins,' said Hannah.

Penelope shook her head. 'I will wait out this night,' she said quietly. 'At least we can pray.'

'Of course he may be guilty,' ventured Hannah cautiously.

'But you do not believe that,' said Penelope.

'N-no. You see, he reminds me of someone.'

'Tell me. It will help to pass the time.'

'I was once a servant,' began Hannah, 'in a large household, Thornton Hall, in Kensington. I do not wish you to tell anyone of this, Miss Wilkins. Can you imagine how such as Miss Trenton would behave towards me? In any case, it all happened when I was a scullery maid. That is how I started in service. Food had been found to be missing from the larder, and somehow this young footman was accused of taking it. He looked a little like Benjamin, not the usual handsome lump of a fellow like your ordinary footman. He was quick and alert and bright. But he made fun of his betters behind their backs and the other servants did not like this.'

'Why?' asked Penelope, round-eyed.

'There is a very strict pecking order in the servants' hall, and above all, your masters must be spoken of with respect. The footman was called Adam. Well, Adam was accused of taking the food and the matter was about to be put before our employers, the Clarences, and I was appalled that a man could be found guilty without any evidence. It was simply because his face and manner did not fit. He was the strange animal in our meek little herd of obedient servants. I slept at nights then under the kitchen table. One night, I decided to stay awake, which was a great effort, for usually I was too tired at the end of the day to keep my eyes open. But I managed this night. At two in the morning, I heard a sound from the larder. There was one of the maids, a sharp-faced girl called Nancy. The kitchen was lit by shafts of moonlight. I stayed in the shadows and she did not see me. She took a large meat-pie and wrapped it in a cloth. Then she went to the back kitchen door and opened it and handed the pie to a villainous-looking ruffian. I said nothing. I went back to my bed and fell asleep. In the morning at the servants' breakfast, the butler announced he was going to report the theft that very day to Mr Clarence. I stood up, feeling very nervous and shaky, sick almost with fright, and told them about Nancy. Nancy threw her apron over her head and began to cry and confessed all. The villain was her brother, a bad lot from Hammersmith, who had threatened her with violence if she did not supply him with food. So that matter was taken to the Clarences, although it was Mrs Clarence who handled the matter.'

'And was Nancy dismissed?' asked Penelope.

'No, for Mrs Clarence was as kind as she was beautiful. She had several of the outside staff wait the next night and they caught the villain. He was told that if he was found within the grounds again, he would be turned over to the magistrate. Nancy became a very willing and obedient servant after that.'

'And Adam?'

'Oh, he left. I do not know what became of him. The other servants did not apologize to him, you know. In fact, I think they blamed him for *not* being the thief. Servants, like other people, are suspicious of anyone whose face does not fit. And yet I liked him. He was not malicious about his employers, only very funny. I think he found service demeaning and it was his way of coping with it. Benjamin reminds me of Adam. I feel he had never been a servant before his employment with Mrs Carsey, but I also feel, whatever he worked at before, it was honest employ.'

Hannah fell silent. She prayed that Lord Augustus would return with some proof of either innocence or guilt before morning. But she did not like to tell Penelope that she had very little hope of his doing so. Lord Augustus, she was convinced, was pleasuring himself in the bed of Lady Carsey and had forgotten all about the footman.

At five in the morning, Lord Augustus crept from Lady Carsey's bed and as softly as a cat began to prowl about the room, looking in boxes and drawers. He felt shaky and exhausted. What a night! At one point he had begun to despair of ever tiring her out. He felt soiled and dirty in mind and body. She was an evil woman, and, he had learned, mad in a vicious way. The light from a tall candle shone across Lady Carsey's body. She was lying on her back, with her mouth slightly open. He searched quickly and rapidly. Where could she have hidden it? He doubted whether she had thrown it away. He had quickly learned she was avaricious. And then he wondered whether she might after all just have left it in her jewel box. The servants seemed to be her creatures, and besides, only her lady's maid other than herself would know if the brooch was still there. He tried the lid of her jewel box. It was locked. He searched in his coat, which he had slung over the back of a chair, until he found a penknife. He slid the blade under the lock. It was not very strong and snapped open with a crack. He waited. The figure on the bed said something and stirred. Then there was a gentle snore. He opened the lid and began to lift out the trays of brooches and necklaces. And there, at the very bottom of the box, he found it – a diamond brooch, oblong and with an edging of sapphires.

Lord Augustus thought quickly. If he awoke her and accused her of her perfidy, she would have time to hide the brooch again, and it would only be his word against hers. If he took the brooch to the authorities, she might claim it was a twin of the one of the footman had taken and accuse him, too, of theft.

He dressed very quickly and let himself softly out of the room and then out of the Manor. Penelope and Hannah would not have recognized the indolent Lord Augustus in the figure that fled down the drive as if all the demons in hell were after him. He ran at great speed straight to the prison and roused the guards and the governor, demanding that a constable and magistrate should come to the Manor with him immediately.

Lady Carsey awoke and stretched like a cat. She rolled over in bed but felt no warm body in the bed beside her. She yawned and sat up. The bedhangings were drawn back and a candle burned and flickered in its stick. Her sleepy eyes fell on the jewel box, which lay on her toilet table with the lid thrown back.

She swung her legs out of bed and stood up just as the door of her bedchamber was flung open and Lord Augustus, followed by the magistrate, the constable, and the governor of the prison, burst into the room.

* * *

Benjamin Stubbs was led out of his prison cell and then out to the gallows. It was five minutes to six in the morning, and he was to hang at six. Only a small group of townspeople had gathered to see the hanging. Hangings were such an everyday event that few troubled to rouse themselves to watch. But Hannah and Penelope were there, clutching hold of each other, their eyes weary with lack of sleep.

'You should not be here,' said Hannah to Penelope. 'There is nothing we can do now.'

'I cannot, I will not, believe that Lord Augustus should abandon us in this shameless way,' said Penelope. 'My papa is always saying the aristocracy are lazy and effete. Why does he then want me to marry one of them? The world is a stupid, wicked place.'

Benjamin mounted the scaffold. His face was white and tense, his eyes bleak. He looked down and saw Hannah and Penelope and made them a stiff bow.

'Look the other way, Penelope,' urged Hannah. 'God grant me the strength, for when he hangs, I am going to jump on that scaffold and pull his legs so his neck will break and it at least will be quick.'

The prison chaplain read a doleful sermon. The rope was put around Benjamin's neck.

'Hold hard!' shouted a voice.

Everyone swung around.

Lord Augustus, the magistrate, the prison governor, and the constable came hurrying up to the scaffold. 'Release the prisoner!' shouted the governor. 'He is innocent.'

Benjamin looked dazed. But then, Hannah thought, how could a deaf man know he had been miraculously reprieved?

'Write it down,' shrieked Penelope. In a shaky hand, Hannah scribbled, 'You are a Free Man.' She climbed the scaffold as the executioner removed the rope from around Benjamin's neck. Four flaring pine torches were burning at each corner of the scaffold. Benjamin held the paper up and read what was written on it.

Then he slowly sank down on one knee and raised the hem of Hannah's dress to his lips.

'Enough of that!' cried Hannah. 'I am not your saviour. It is Lord Augustus you should thank. Oh, of course, you cannot hear a word I am saying.' She wrote it down. Benjamin rose and read it. He shook his head in bewilderment.

Hannah Pym took his hand in hers and then, as if leading a child, she took him down from the scaffold.

3

Though in silence, with blighted affection, I pine,
Yet the lips that touch liquor must never touch mine!

G.W. Young

The departure of the stage-coach was delayed while the formalities of securing Benjamin's release were gone through.

Miss Trenton was incensed, so much so that the glory of Lord Augustus's title faded in her eyes. For once her sympathies almost seemed to be with Penelope. His lordship sat at his ease in front of the inn fire with the magistrate and laconically went over his statement. Penelope was listening, round-eyed. Yes, said Lord Augustus, he had bedded Lady Carsey and deuced exhausting it had been, too, but all in the interests of justice, don't you know. The magistrate, an elderly man, said severely that although saving an innocent man from the gallows was commendable, his methods were deplorable. Unrepentant, Lord Augustus pointed out that there did not seem to be any other way of obtaining proof.

'Indeed!' said the magistrate severely. 'Would it not have been better to have put your suspicions before me, my lord, and then we could have obtained a warrant and made a search?'

'Tish,' said Lord Augustus, half closing his eyes. 'I can see it all now. You arrive at the Manor with the warrant but full of obsequious apologies. My lady would have been all help and compliance. She would have ordered her maid to fetch her jewel box and the maid, already knowing her mistress had lied, would have hidden the brooch where it could never be found. I have made my statement and am weary of this town and wish to be on my way.'

'As you will,' said the magistrate, removing his glasses and stowing them away with fussy care in a shagreen case. 'But Lady Carsey is a well-respected member of this town, my lord. I am convinced she made an innocent mistake.'

He rose to his feet, gathered his papers, and walked out.

'Heigh-ho!' said Lord Augustus. 'Thank goodness that's over. What becomes of our Benjamin?'

Hannah fumbled in her reticule and took out two guineas and handed them to Benjamin. He pushed them away and stared at her in mute appeal.

'He wants to write something,' said Penelope. 'Give him a piece of paper.'

Hannah took out her notebook and gave it to Benjamin. He wrote busily and then handed it back to her. She read, 'I wish to be Yr. Servant. No wages. Food will be enough.'

'What does he want?' asked Mr Cato.

'He wants to be my servant.'

Miss Trenton tittered and then said in a shrill voice, 'The impertinence of the fellow. Of course you must refuse. In my opinion, Lady Carsey knew something about him which led her to believe he took that brooch.'

'He would be better to register at one of the agencies and go out to America as a bonded servant,' said Mr Cato. 'I'll arrange it for the fellow.'

Benjamin kept his eyes fixed on Hannah.

'I could employ him for a little,' said Hannah slowly, 'that is, until I find a position somewhere for him.' She thought of Sir George. Surely he would have enough connections to find work for one footman.

'May I point out,' said Lord Augustus meekly, 'that our coachman is waiting and I am anxious to be shot of this place.'

Hannah made up her mind. She would purchase a seat for Benjamin on the stage. She thought ruefully of her dwindling finances. It would need to be an inside seat, for it had begun to rain and Benjamin was dressed only in a thin, torn shirt and breeches.

'Perhaps,' said Hannah, 'someone might be so good as to go to the Manor to collect Benjamin's clothes?' She looked at Lord Augustus.

'Not I, ma'am,' he said, raising his hands in mock horror. 'I never want to see that place again.'

'Are you all coming aboard or ain't you?' growled the coachman.

Hannah wrote in the notebook, 'I shall purchase you a seat inside on the stage. You may stay with me for only a little. I shall find you employ when we return to London.'

She stood up. Benjamin leaped to his feet and deftly picked up Hannah's shawl and reticule and stood to attention behind her.

She went off to the booking-office in the inn and bought the ticket. Miss Trenton let out a squawk of sheer fury when she realized that Benjamin was to sit with the insiders. 'How dare you, Miss Pym,' she raged. 'A carriage lady such as myself is not going to travel in the company of *that*.'

'Stow it, you old crow,' said Mr Cato in a sudden passion. 'I have to reach my ship before she sails. If I hear one more word of that carriage of yours, I'll scream. You ain't got no carriage and we all know it.'

'*Well*.' Miss Trenton bridled. But she climbed on board the coach, although her face, or what could be seen of it inside her bonnet, was quite pink with outrage.

Hannah sat in her corner seat with Benjamin beside her. Penelope sat opposite with Lord Augustus next to her, and Miss Trenton and Mr Cato faced each other over on the other side of the coach. Miss Trenton's disapproval filled the carriage.

But after less than a mile, Benjamin, Hannah, Penelope, and Lord Augustus fell asleep. They did not

45

even awake three miles and four furlongs down the road when the coach made a brief stop at Cobham. Only Mr Cato and Miss Trenton were awake to accept the offered glasses of rum and hot milk.

Three miles, seven furlongs farther on, and they were at Ripley, famous for its cricketers, and its old inn, the Talbot, full of gables and long corridors. The coachman jerked open the door, but by now all the passengers were asleep, so he fortified himself with brandy and drove on. Seven miles on, and the coach rolled to a stop in the sleepy town of Guildford. The passengers struggled awake and silently and sleepily filed into the Crown.

Although Benjamin was standing at attention behind Hannah's chair, the landlord took one look at his dirty and unshaven face and tried to turn him out. Lord Augustus took the landlord aside and said something, and after that there was no complaint. But Lord Augustus murmured to Hannah, 'We stop here for but a short while. Perhaps there might be somewhere in the town where you can purchase a livery for your new servant.'

Hannah got to her feet, signalling to Benjamin to stay where he was. 'Make sure the coach does not leave without me,' she said, and hurried out.

'Now that is a resourceful lady,' said Lord Augustus. 'More ham, Miss Wilkins?'

Penelope murmured, 'No,' and would not meet his eyes.

Penelope had a lot to think about. She was a dutiful daughter and admired her father very much and dreaded his disappointment when he learned she had been expelled from the seminary. When she had first seen Lord Augustus, although she had not fallen in love with him, she had thought of marriage. How pleased her father would be if she married a lord! Lord Augustus seemed a dilettante, but an easygoing and comfortable one. Then, when it seemed that he might be prepared to help Benjamin, her imagination had quickly raised him up to new heights and credited him with all sorts of noble attributes. When it looked as if he had no intention of saving the servant, she had damned him as totally useless. But now he *had* saved Benjamin, but in such a way! When it came to love-making, Penelope's imagination through lack of practical knowledge did not go much further than kissing and hugging. She had first assumed Lord Augustus had been exhausted by his night with Lady Carsey because he had talked all night long in an effort to try to get her to believe Benjamin's innocence. But when Lord Augustus had been telling the magistrate of his adventures, not only the magistrate but everyone else had looked shocked. Therefore it followed that Lord Augustus must have made love to Lady Carsey, and nowhere in the romances Penelope read did a hero make carnal love to a woman he obviously disliked. So Lord Augustus, she decided, belonged to a wicked and decadent world to which she did not want to belong. The other girls in the seminary had whispered of scandals, of how one must marry well, but how, if one was discreet, one could take a lover after marriage. All this had not sat easily in Penelope's puritan mind. To date, she had mostly lived through books. Her father, although a self-made man and a Radical, had kept her away from her peers in the merchant class of Portsmouth. Penelope's mother, a small, quiet lady whose faded looks only occasionally showed that she had once boasted the same beauty as her daughter, obeyed her husband in every respect. Penelope had followed her mother's lead, but now she felt the first stirrings of rebellion. What was wrong with the merchant class? She herself admired men who worked. Lord Augustus was travelling on the stage only because he had obviously gambled all his money away and was now hoping to coerce his aged uncle into either giving him some or to leaving him money in his will. She also thought that he drank too much. It was a hard drinking age, and yet Penelope had grown to despise drunken men and had no intention of marrying one.

Unaware that Lord Augustus was watching her, Penelope's face hardened. She raised her eyes at last, found Lord Augustus watching her, and quickly veiled them, but not before he had seen the slight contempt in her eyes.

Lord Augustus was normally an easygoing man. But that look of contempt he had just surprised in Penelope's eyes irritated him greatly. Had he not, for her sake, bedded a repulsive woman? He ignored a niggling voice in his head that told him that he would probably have done it anyway, for Benjamin's plight had touched him as much as it had touched Hannah and Penelope. He thought haughtily that Penelope was, after all, a trifle common with her little snub nose and total lack of the arts to please. And yet her very innocence and virginity struck him like a reproach.

Hannah returned, slightly out of breath, with a package that she handed to Benjamin. She took out her notebook and wrote, 'Put these on and join me in the coach.'

Benjamin bowed and took the package. 'I was lucky in finding a good second-hand clothes-shop,' said Hannah to Penelope.

The small group of passengers filed out and boarded the coach and then patiently waited for Hannah's footman. 'Are we never to move? Are we to sit here all day waiting for this criminal to favour us with his presence?' demanded Miss Trenton acidly.

The carriage door opened at that moment and Benjamin climbed inside, although it took all a few moments to realize it *was* Benjamin. He was wearing a suit of black-and-gold livery. His hair was powdered. He had washed and shaved and seemed very proud of his appearance.

Lord Augustus studied Benjamin covertly as the carriage moved on. The man was too bright and intelligent to be a servant. Lord Augustus doubted that Benjamin had ever been a servant before his brief stay with Lady Carsey. Footmen were often effeminate and lazy. There was an air of cheekiness and independence about Benjamin. How old was he? Lord Augustus thought he was probably in his late twenties and had lived on his wits for quite some time. He wondered, too, whether Benjamin was really deaf and dumb or had heard of Lady Carsey's predeliction for 'freaks' and was only affecting to be so.

'Benjamin!' he said suddenly.

The footman turned his head sharply in his direction. 'So you *can* hear,' said Lord Augustus.

Benjamin shook his head and then tugged at Hannah's sleeve. She handed him the notebook. He wrote something down and gave it to Lord Augustus.

'So you say you can read lips,' said Lord Augustus. 'A useful talent. Would you not say so, Miss Wilkins?'

'No, I do not think so,' replied Penelope after some moments' thought. 'One would know what people on the other side of a room were saying about one. It would be like listening at doors.'

Hannah stifled a sigh. There would be no matchmaking for her on this journey. Mr Wilkins would need to train his daughter in the social arts if he wished to realize his ambitions. Obviously no one had ever taught Penelope that a young lady *never* corrects a gentleman.

Lord Augustus was thinking the same thing. The more he thought about Penelope as the journey progressed, the more she irritated him. After he had served six long years in the army, he had become weary of war and bloodshed and had decided that a life devoted to pleasure was the only answer. And to date it had worked very well. He had gambled, and raced and flirted and danced and drunk deep with like-minded cronies. He was a younger son, on a younger son's allowance. He would not inherit any estates or responsibilities. He did not want to go to war again, and the Church of England bored him. The navy he considered even more barbaric than the army, and he was prone to seasickness. But he was not going to consider his life a dreary desert and a total waste of time because one little bourgeoise disapproved of him. And was she so innocent? After all, she must surely have known her music teacher was smitten by her. She could easily have depressed his courting before it got too far.

The coach stopped briefly at Godalming. Penelope, Lord Augustus noticed sourly, refused rum and milk and asked for a glass of water instead.

The coach then started out on the long five-mile climb to the top of Hindhead. The timbers of the coach creaked alarmingly, like a very old ship on a high sea.

'I do not trust the repairs,' said Mr Cato suddenly. 'Cobbled together, no doubt. We should have waited at Esher until the company sent another coach.'

But the coach breasted the top of the hill without incident. It was all downhill to Liphook, and the coach began to gather speed to make up for lost time. It swayed and jolted alarmingly. Miss Trenton squealed with fright. Two miles down the hill, there came an enormous crack, followed by the splintering of wood.

Then they were all thrown forward. Hannah fell on top of Penelope, Benjamin on top of Lord Augustus. Mr Cato and Miss Trenton lay as close as lovers in a heap on the floor. The poles of the coach had snapped.

Miss Trenton began to cry. It was an odd sound, like a courting cat, 'Yow! Yewow! Yow!'

'Stow it,' shouted Mr Cato. The coach was tilted forward at a crazy angle. Lord Augustus wrenched open the door and climbed out. The coachman lay sprawled at the side of the road, dangerously near the kicking and thrashing of the frightened horses' hooves. Lord Augustus ran to him. He was unconscious. The guard struggled around the side of the coach, cursing the villain who had sawn it up in Esher and cursing the repairman who had done such a disastrously bad job.

Lord Augustus knelt down by the coachman and loosened his neckcloth. Hannah climbed out of the wrecked coach, helped by Benjamin, and then both assisted Penelope to alight. Then appeared Mr Cato, who leaned back in and tugged out Miss Trenton. Her yowls reduced to sobs, Miss Trenton sat down on the ground and buried her face in her hands.

Her horrible bonnet had come off during the accident, revealing her small, pinched, discontented face topped with masses of luxuriant red hair. It was not sandy like Hannah's, but a flaming glorious red, an improbable colour for such a withered spinster to flaunt.

Lord Augustus decided sourly that Miss Trenton was behaving just as a lady ought, given the circumstances. His next thought was that he was being stupid. Surely it was better to have the competent and brisk Miss Pym and the calm and beautiful Penelope than to have the whole lot of them screaming and wailing. That was followed by a brief flicker of an idea that it would have been pleasant to soothe a distressed Penelope.

He went to the horses' heads and calmed them, glad they were miraculously unhurt. He wondered at his own reckless folly in damaging the coach in the first place and thought ruefully of various silly pranks he had played in London with his drunken friends. He unhitched one of the leaders and then cut the rest free from the traces and tethered them to a couple of gateposts beside the road. He mounted the leader and rode off down the hill for help.

'He is really very competent,' said Penelope thoughtfully.

'Yes, very,' said Hannah Pym, giving a tug to her crooked nose and throwing Penelope a sideways look. 'I think his idle life has not given him a chance to exercise his talents. Perhaps what he needs is a good woman.'

'I do not think so,' said Penelope.

'Why, pray?' demanded Hannah in an irritated voice, for she was still hoping to make a match between the unlikely pair.

Penelope gurgled with laughter. 'I think he needs the love of a *bad* woman. Anyone else would bore him and drive him from home.'

'*I* think,' said Mr Cato acidly, 'that instead of discussing our absent friend, you ladies might lend a little help in soothing Miss Trenton.'

'We have *all* had a fright,' said Hannah repressively. 'Thank goodness we are not still carrying outsiders, or one of them might have been seriously hurt.'

Benjamin, who was carrying Hannah's reticule, fished in it and produced a vinaigrette that he held under Miss Trenton's nose. The attention rather than the smell seemed to rally her. Then she clutched her head with a wail. 'My bonnet!'

Benjamin bowed and went into the coach and then emerged carrying the bonnet. Hannah looked at her footman sharply. For the bonnet was not only crushed but looked as if it had just been jumped on.

Miss Trenton began to yowl and moan again. 'Heavens!' snapped Hannah. 'If you have not another hat in your luggage, you may have one of mine.'

'My hair,' said Miss Trenton when she could.

'What is up with it?'

'It is *red*!'

'And a very fine colour, too, you stupid woman,' expostulated Mr Cato.

But Hannah and Penelope looked at the stricken Miss Trenton sympathetically. Red hair was highly unfashionable, the Scottish race being prone to that colour, and the Scots had not yet been forgiven, not only for the rebellion of '45, but for travelling to the south in great numbers and taking all the best jobs, or so the prejudice claimed.

'It is not ordinary,' said Hannah bracingly. 'Now, my hair is sandy, and not at all the thing. But yours, Miss Trenton, is of great beauty. You should not hide it.'

Miss Trenton put a shaky hand up to arrange her tumbled tresses.

Benjamin had found a carriage rug, made a pillow of it and put it under the coachman's head. The wind howled mournfully about them and great ragged clouds tumbled across the sky.

Mr Cato fetched other rugs and spread them on the grass beside the road and everyone sat down and waited for Lord Augustus to return with help.

'I hate this climate,' said Mr Cato passionately. 'I wish I were back home.'

'Home will surely be England,' said Miss Trenton. 'You Americans will come to your senses soon enough.'

'We came to our senses in '76,' growled Mr Cato.

'Were you born in America?' asked Hannah curiously.

'No, I was in Bristol and a good and loyal subject to King George. I went out as a bonded servant. Worked as groom to Mr Josiah Baxter, a tobacco planter. He took kindly to me and when my seven years were up, he trained me in the working of the plantations. Soon I began to see why the colonists had rebelled.'

'Taxes?' asked Penelope.

'Geography,' replied Mr Cato succinctly. 'It's so big, America. So vast. So free. After a bit, England seems small and grubby and petty.'

'And yet you have slaves,' snapped Hannah, who could not bear to hear such criticism.

'I'm a good master. I see them all right,' growled Mr Cato. 'You in England dirty your hands with the trading of them. Don't come hoity-toity with me, ma'am.'

'And yet you came back,' pointed out Hannah. 'Why?'

Mr Cato's red face became even redder. 'That's my affair.' He rounded on Miss Trenton. 'Bad manners in you, Miss Trenton, to claim to be so ashamed of red hair when I have a quantity of the stuff myself.'

'It's different for a man,' said Miss Trenton. 'Men do not need to look beautiful.'

'How I wish Lord Augustus would come back,' said Penelope hurriedly to avert a row. 'It is tedious waiting here.'

Benjamin produced hazard dice from his pocket and began to roll them on the ground. Mr Cato's eyes gleamed. The guard edged closer. Hannah scribbled frantically on a piece of paper, 'I will not tolerate gambling,' and tried to pass it to Benjamin but found the paper twitched out of her hand by Mr Cato. 'Don't stop him,' said the American. 'Best way to pass the time.'

Hannah rose to her feet. She would deal with Benjamin later. 'Walk with me, Miss Wilkins.' Penelope obediently got up and they walked a little way away from the coach.

'Are all men in London society like Lord Augustus?' asked Penelope.

'No,' said Hannah. 'Quite a number of them are ill-featured and few are so amiable.'

'But such a wasted life!'

'My dear Miss Wilkins, Lord Augustus was not bred to work unless he chooses the military or the Church. Where did you come by such odd notions?'

'My father.' Penelope gave a little sigh. 'I declare I was quite shocked when he sent me to the seminary and told me I must be groomed for a Season so that I could catch a title.'

'Even the most radical of parents becomes ambitious when he finds himself with a pretty daughter.'

'I am pretty in a common way,' said Penelope reflectively. 'They told me that at the seminary. It is the nose, you see. I lie in bed sometimes and dream that when I awake, I will find I have sprouted a patrician nose during the night. My mouth also is a trifle big. Miss Jasper went on – Miss Jasper at the seminary, that is – as if my mouth were all *my* fault. She made me say my Prunes and Prisms by the hour.' Penelope pursed her lips. 'Bit it is seh hird to tuck.'

'Then do not try to talk with your mouth screwed up. You have a very pretty mouth.'

'Someone's coming,' said Penelope.

Sure enough, Lord Augustus appeared riding the leader and followed by inn servants and two post-chaises.

He swung himself down from the saddle and said, 'The landlord of the Thorn Tree is ready and waiting for us. How is our coachman?'

As if in reply, the coachman stirred and mumbled. Lord Augustus knelt down beside him and held a flask of brandy to his lips. The coachman feebly drank some and seized the flask from Lord Augustus's hand and took a great swig and then struggled up with a groan.

'He'll do,' said Lord Augustus cheerfully, relieved that he no longer was plagued with the vision of a dangerously injured coachman on his conscience. 'In the carriages, everyone.'

Benjamin pocketed his dice. He was looking very pleased with himself while the guard looked sullen and Mr Cato furious.

The Thorn Tree was quickly reached. Everything had been arranged for them. Bedchambers had been aired, fires lit, and the landlord said that dinner would be served directly. A physician arrived to attend to the coachman.

To Hannah's embarrassment, Benjamin entered her room and began to take out her clothes and underthings and put them away. Odd to be so embarrassed when she had been a servant herself.

'I wish you could talk or even hear what I am saying,' grumbled Hannah aloud. 'I would like to talk to you, Benjamin, for I am tired of writing notes. This is my third journey on the Flying Machine, and on the two previous journeys, I pride myself that I was instrumental in making matches for two couples . . . three,' she added, thinking of a certain widow and a shabby lawyer. 'But there is no scope on this journey. Even if Miss Wilkins should form a *tendresse* for Lord Augustus, it would not answer. That father of hers thinks he wants a lord for a son-in-law, but what would he make of the indolent Lord Augustus? And Miss Wilkins has been raised in too plebeian, well, normal, a background to understand a husband who might have affairs and whose whole life is given over to the pursuit of fur, feather, and female. Why, what is this, Benjamin?'

58

The footman had pulled a handful of silver and copper out of his pocket and was holding it out to her. He mimed shaking and throwing dice and thrust the money at her.

Hannah sighed and took out her notebook and wrote that she did not approve of gambling and could not therefore take his winnings. Benjamin threw her a scornful look and thrust the money at her again.

Hannah capitulated. 'Very well, Benjamin, I will keep it for your board, for I am not wealthy.' She eyed him narrowly. 'You appear to understand what I say!'

Benjamin mimed that he could read lips. 'I had forgot that,' exclaimed Hannah, looking relieved. She faced him squarely and said, 'So if I look at you direct and say something, you will understand me?'

The footman nodded vigorously.

'Well, that's a mercy. Leave me until I change my gown.'

Penelope in her bedchamber took out a delicate gown of pink India muslin and put it on. The inn was warm, and therefore it would be possible to wear one of those dreadfully scanty creations, so fashionable in 1800. Odd, mused Penelope, that Miss Jasper, so strict in all things, had bowed to fashion and had not even raised an eyebrow when Penelope and the other girls marched to church with the hems of their gowns looped over their arms, showing delectable visions of pink-silk-clad legs.

She brushed her hair until it shone, wishing her hair had a more definite colour than a kind of duskiness, neither black nor brown. But it had a natural curl and she never had to suffer the discomfort of sleeping in curl-papers.

Lord Augustus paused in the corridor as Penelope left her bedchamber. She turned and looked up at him, her eyes wide. He caught his breath. She was so very young and so very beautiful. High-fashion sticklers might damn her nose but Lord Augustus reflected it gave an appealing kittenish air to her face. Her bosom was beautifully formed and quite a bit of it was revealed by the low cut of her gown. He felt his senses quicken.

'Why do you stare at me so?' said the vision crossly. 'Have I a smut on my nose?'

He sighed. The vision was cursed with plain-speaking to a fault. Ladies were supposed to blush and lower their eyes under his admiring gaze.

'Yes,' he said, and strolled off down the corridor. Penelope let out a squawk of dismay and dived back into her room.

She appeared at the dinner-table shortly after Lord Augustus and glared at him. 'I did not have a smut on my nose,' she said.

'The corridor was dim,' drawled Lord Augustus. 'Possibly it was a shadow thrown on your face by one of these huge spiders which seem to infest this inn.'

Miss Trenton screamed in horror. Hannah gave Lord Augustus a reproachful look, and Penelope said scornfully, 'I have not seen one spider in this inn.'

Benjamin was standing behind Hannah's chair. She looked at the delicious meal spread in front of them and wished she could ask Benjamin to sit down and join them, but that would be worse than inviting an outside passenger to the table. The coachman, fully recovered, could be seen through in the tap, drinking brandy with the guard.

'The men are working on the coach now,' said Mr Cato. 'Coachee says we'll be off in the morning. B'Gad, if I miss my ship, I shall charge the coach company for whatever expenses I may incur in waiting in Portsmouth for another. You do not eat, Miss Trenton.'

Miss Trenton, who had found a muslin cap to wear over her flaming hair, simpered and said, 'I have an appetite like a bird.' And so she did, thought Hannah, amazed, as the meal progressed. A vulture. As was the fashion of the day, all the courses were served at once. The diners helped themselves to whatever they fancied, one plate doing for everything. They had stewed lamb, fresh young codling, steamed cabbage, pork, a large turbot, mussels, roast veal, a heap of cress, potatoes in thick brown sauce, and a salad and pastries. Miss Trenton put a tiny amount on her plate and as soon as the others had started to eat, she put a large helping of everything in front of her and demolished it with amazing rapidity.

Lord Augustus was seated next to Penelope. He was sharply aware of her, bemused to find that what had been a rather common and tiresome female earlier in the day had mysteriously become an enchantress to stir his blood. He could hardly take his eyes off her, off the turn of her dimpled arm as she raised the wineglass to her soft lips, off the glory of an errant curl that lay against the whiteness of one shoulder.

Only Miss Trenton, chewing and swallowing assi-duously, noticed Lord Augustus's new preoccupation with Penelope and felt the sour bile of jealousy beginning to spoil her meal. It was always thus, had always been thus. Her own strength of character and what she considered her own unusual beauty had always been ignored by the gentlemen. She did not, as the other passengers had correctly guessed, have a private carriage. She had been a governess at a seminary in London and had recently lost her post, and all because of a girl such as Penelope. The girl had been a young Miss Coates, rich daughter of a banker, who had tearfully complained to her father that Miss Trent was making her life a misery. Miss Trent had therefore been dismissed. She was travel-ling to Portsmouth because an old friend ran a seminary there and she hoped to find a new post. She had very little money and was glad that Mr Cato seemed prepared to pay her inn bills. Although it was expected that gentlemen in a stage-coach party should pay for the ladies, such was not always the case.

When Lord Augustus raised his glass and smiled down at Penelope and said, 'Will you take wine with me?' Miss Trenton felt a stab of pure fury. Penelope's obvious lack of interest in the noble lord did nothing to allay Miss Trenton's fury. Penelope would return to that father of hers and all would be forgiven. Mr Wilkins would no doubt blame the seminary.

After dinner, Mr Cato surprised the company by saying he would entertain them to a song or two. He started off with,

'There was a maid went to a mill,
Sing trolly, lolly, lolly, lo,
The mill turn'd round but the maid stood still,
Oh, Oh, ho! Oh, ho! Oh, oh! did she so?'

He received some polite applause and went on with,

'Sing dyllum, dyllum, dyllum, dyllum,
I can tell you and I will,
Of my lady's water-mill.'

'Steady on!' cried Lord Augustus in alarm, but Mr Cato was launched on the next verse.

'It was a maid of brenten arse,
She rode to mill upon a horse,
Yet she was a maiden never the worse.'

'Mr Cato!' shouted Lord Augustus, who knew the rest of the song only too well. 'Ladies present!'

Mr Cato looked sheepish. 'Forgot,' he said. 'A million apologies. Not used to the company of ladies. You sing something, my lord.'

Urged on by the others, Lord Augustus rose to his feet. He did not want to sing. He wanted to go on examining the effect Penelope was having on his senses. He chose the first song that came into his head. His clear tenor voice fell with disastrous clarity on the listening ears.

'Yankee Doodle went to town,
He rode a little pony,
He stuck a feather in his hat
And called it macaroni.
Yankee Doodle fa, so, la,
Yankee Doodle dandy.
Yankee Doodle fa, so, la,
Buttermilk and brandy.'

Mr Cato leaped to his feet, his fists swinging. 'You shall answer for that,' he shouted.

Lord Augustus looked at him in horror, realizing for the first time what he had just sung. 'Yankee Doodle', that ballad used by British soldiers to taunt the New Englanders with aspirations to fashion, who thought they looked like Macaronies simply by putting feathers in their hats, and could only afford to ride ponies, had been a slur in '76, but as the years had passed, had simply become a popular ballad. He also realized the infuriated American was quite drunk.

'My apologies,' said Lord Augustus as Mr Cato staggered around the table towards him. 'Fie, sir, we have all had too much to drink. You are not a New Englander. Come, sir. You may sing an American song if you wish.'

Mr Cato stood in front of Lord Augustus. His red face was now so very red he looked about to explode.

'You did, after all, win the war.' Lord Augustus raised his glass. 'A toast! To General George Washington.'

Mr Cato looked bemused. Hannah thrust a glass of wine into his hand.

'General George Washington,' roared everyone.

Mr Cato drank, the fire dying out of his cheeks. Mollified, he said, 'I thought you was making a fool of me, my lord.'

'We have both had a disastrous choice of songs this night. Let the ladies entertain us. Miss Trenton!'

Miss Trenton blushed and disclaimed. She had a poor voice, she said. But urged on, she rose to her feet and sang 'Drink to Me Only' in a surprisingly pretty voice. Mr Cato and Lord Augustus resumed their seats. Miss Trenton was wildly applauded, not so much for the beauty of her singing, but because everyone was relieved that a nasty row had been averted. Mr Cato urged Miss Trenton to take wine with him, and the more wine Miss Trenton drank, the more jealous she became of Penelope.

The party moved their chairs to sit around the fire and Miss Trenton found herself beside Lord Augustus.

'Ahem,' she said, clearing her throat genteelly to catch his attention. 'Sad business about Miss Wilkins.'

Lord Augustus looked amused. 'Being sent home? I think she has a doting father and all will be forgiven.'

'Perhaps not this time,' said Miss Trenton darkly.

He looked at her malicious little eyes and felt he should turn away. But his interest in Penelope was becoming very great. He waited.

'I said nothing at the time,' went on Miss Trenton, 'but I know that seminary in Esher and heard of Miss Wilkins's downfall.'

'Driving some poor music master to behave in a silly way can hardly be called a downfall.'

Miss Trenton leaned closer to Lord Augustus and whispered, 'But Miss Wilkins let the music master have his way with her. The poor man then felt he *had* to propose.'

Lord Augustus turned away from her and began to talk to Hannah while all the time his mind raced. The sensible side of it told him that Miss Trenton was a spiteful spinster. The rakish side of his mind almost wanted to believe her. There was something so, well, sensuous, about Penelope.

He looked across at her to where she sat on the other side of the fireplace. At that moment, Penelope, who had been thinking uneasily about the spiders he had described, thought she felt something crawling over her ankle and raised the hem of her skirt. To Lord Augustus it appeared as if Penelope had deliberately raised her skirts to afford him a glimpse of tantalizing ankles.

Penelope was becoming increasingly aware of Lord Augustus as a man. Despite his air of frivolity and his impeccably tailored clothes, he was undoubtedly very strong and masculine. The firelight played on the strong muscles of his legs stretched out on the hearth. Hannah could have told Penelope that there was nothing more seductive than a man with good legs. Gentleman Jackson, the famous boxer, was hardly an

Adonis, but no one talked about his face; all sighed over the beauty of his legs.

So across the fireplace, the very air between Lord Augustus and Penelope became charged with emotion. Lord Augustus was thinking that perhaps he might try to steal a kiss and see how she reacted.

The party eventually broke up when the coachman reminded them they would all have to set out as early as possible. Repairs on the coach were going on all night.

Lord Augustus quickly moved to Penelope's side. 'Would you care to take the air with me, Miss Wilkins, before retiring?'

'Yes, I would,' said Penelope candidly. 'It is so very stuffy here. I will fetch my cloak.'

She went upstairs. Hannah followed her. 'I am taking a little walk with Lord Augustus,' said Penelope. 'I am sure that is safe enough.'

Hannah hesitated, all hopes of making a match between the pair rushing back into her head. And yet, Penelope should not be unchaperoned.

'What a good idea,' exclaimed Hannah. 'May I come with you?'

'Of course,' said Penelope, relieved at first at the prospect of having a chaperone, and then disappointed.

Lord Augustus quickly masked *his* disappointment when he found Hannah was to accompany them. They all walked out into the inn yard.

The wind was still blowing but it held a certain warmth, a hint of spring. Lord Augustus drew

Penelope's arm through his own. Penelope felt suddenly shy and tongue-tied and worried by the surge of emotions in her body caused by that pressure of his arm. Her knees were beginning to tremble and something seemed to have happened to her breath.

'Hold hard!' cried Hannah suddenly. 'I thought I saw two men lurking by the gate!'

Lord Augustus released Penelope and darted forward. He looked up and down the road outside the inn-gate but could not see anyone. He turned back. 'The wind is blowing through the trees at the side of the road and casting moving shadows, Miss Pym.'

'Perhaps,' said Hannah uneasily.

'I am going indoors,' said Penelope. 'It is cold.' And she hurried before them to the inn, afraid that Lord Augustus would take her arm again and cause all that sickening tumult in her body.

4

Lord! I wonder what fool it was that first invented kissing!

Jonathan Swift

Hannah Pym felt she was getting spoiled. Although the breakfast hour was early, six o'clock, in fact, she had not expected Benjamin to sleep in. But he had not presented himself at her bedchamber door to carry her trunk, and she had had to ring for, and therefore tip, the waiter. There were the stage-coach passengers around the table when she went downstairs, but no footman.

When they rose to leave the inn and take their places in the now repaired coach, Hannah sent a waiter upstairs to rouse Benjamin from his bed in a cheap attic room. She then went out with the others and climbed into the carriage. Lack of punctuality in servants Hannah regarded as a sin. When she had been housekeeper to Mr Clarence, no servant under her rule dared to lie abed. She cursed herself for her soft-hearted folly in taking on Benjamin. What need had she of a servant?

The waiter poked his head in the coach window and remarked laconically that there was 'no sign of the fellow'.

'Made a run for it,' commented Mr Cato, shaking his head wisely. 'Better check your goods, ma'am.'

'No need for that,' remarked Hannah impatiently. 'I packed everything myself.'

A blast from the guard's horn sounded from the roof of the coach. The waiter backed away.

'Wait!' shouted Hannah, thrusting her head out of the window. 'Hold, I say!'

She climbed out of the coach and called up to the coachman, 'My servant is missing. Be so good as to wait a few moments.' And before the coachman could reply, Hannah picked up her skirts and ran towards the inn.

It was as the waiter had said. Benjamin's little room was empty. Hannah stood, irresolute, strangely reluctant to believe her footman had run off and left her.

And then she saw a dark stain on the floor. She picked up a candle and lit it after some fumbling with a tinder-box and then held it close to the stain.

She put a finger down to the mark and then examined it.

Blood.

Her heart began to hammer. Carrying the candle, she inspected the narrow uncarpeted staircase closely. There were long scuff-marks on the treads and more marks of blood.

Blowing out the candle, she placed it on the floor and hurtled down the stairs, out of the inn and up to the coach. She wrenched open the door and cried, 'Benjamin was attacked during the night and taken.'

Lord Augustus, who had been half-asleep, opened his eyes. 'Are you sure?'

'Oh yes, my lord.' She told him of the blood-stains on the floor and stairs and of the scuff-marks, which looked as if they had been made by Benjamin's heels as his body was dragged from the room.

The coach dipped and swayed as the coachman climbed down to find out what was causing the delay. 'Then if you wish to speak to the authorities about your servant,' said Miss Trenton, 'you may wait behind.'

'It has something to do with Lady Carsey,' said Penelope suddenly. 'I know it. I feel it *here.*'

She put a hand to her bosom. Lord Augustus immediately wondered what it would be like to put his own hand there and then quickly damned the fair Penelope for conjuring up erotic thoughts on a bleak morning.

Hannah looked at Lord Augustus appealingly. 'What am I to do?' she asked.

'Good Heavens,' he said languidly. 'Take note of this. The redoubtable Miss Pym at a loss.'

The coachman angrily demanded to know what was going on. Hannah explained. The coachman said

71

crossly that it was all a bad business but they had to be moving forward.

'Stay,' said Penelope. 'Miss Pym must not be left with this great worry. I shall stay with you, Miss Pym.'

'It ain't all that very far to Esher,' said Mr Cato suddenly.

'My thoughts exactly,' said Lord Augustus. 'But what of your ship?'

'With all these delays,' snapped Mr Cato, 'it'll be a miracle if it's still there.'

Miss Trenton was almost gasping with outrage. 'Are you proposing to take this coach back to Esher in pursuit of one shoddy footman?'

Lord Augustus looked at Penelope's beseeching eyes. 'Why, yes, ma'am, that is it in a nutshell.'

'Lookee here,' said the coachman. 'What do I tell the company when they find I've put yet another day on the journey?'

'You tell them that the repairs took a day longer,' said Lord Augustus equably.

'It's all very fine for you to talk, my lord,' said the coachman. 'But what if I loses me job?'

Lord Augustus drew off his gloves and put one white hand up to the lace at his throat. He plucked out a fine sapphire pin and held it up for a moment to the light. 'All my pretty baubles,' he sighed. 'And I did think this suited the colour of my eyes so well; did not you, Miss Wilkins?'

Penelope said nothing, merely clasped her hands tightly and stared at him, her eyes enormous in her face.

'There you are, coachman,' said Lord Augustus. 'Esher it is.'

The coachman took the pin, his eyes gleaming. 'Right you are, my lord. Reckon as how the old coach will hold fast. Right good job they did this time.'

'I shall write to the company,' screamed Miss Trenton, beside herself with rage. She had found a small, dainty hat to wear on her flaming hair, but it showed the full fury of her face.

'Be quiet, you,' roared Mr Cato.

Miss Trenton shrank back in her seat and began to snivel. Mr Cato surveyed her coldly and then handed her a large handkerchief like a bed-sheet, saying in a milder tone, 'I appreciate your distress, Miss Trenton, for you are the only one among us who don't seem made for adventures, and I guess that is why you are still a maid.'

This remark had the effect of shocking Miss Trenton into complete silence. Hannah returned to the inn to question the landlord and servants, but no one had seen or heard anything strange during the night. She told the others of her lack of success at finding any information as the coach swung out on the long road back to Esher.

The passengers, with the exception of Miss Trenton, who was not consulted, agreed to remain in the coach, even when the horses were being changed, and to have their refreshment brought out to them. The sun rose on another windy day, and as they approached Esher, they fell to discussing what to do. Mr Cato was all for going to the magistrate. Lord

Augustus said they had no proof. Benjamin's body might already be lying dead in some ditch or, if he were still alive, he might be at the Manor, lying in some cellar.

'She has to have her revenge,' he said. 'She's that sort.'

Penelope looked at him, remembered his love-making to Lady Carsey, and blushed and turned her face away.

'So what are we to do?' demanded Mr Cato.

'For a start,' said Lord Augustus slowly, 'I do not think we should go into Esher itself but rack up at some wayside inn before we reach there. Otherwise, she will quickly learn of our return. We will find a place for the night. I shall tell the coachman of our plans.' At the next stop where they changed horses again, Lord Augustus instructed the coachman to find some wayside inn outside Esher.

They left the main road before they reached the town and went along a country lane, the coachman eventually stopping at what looked to Miss Trenton's jaundiced eye like a hedge-tavern.

She was still complaining that a lady of the carriage class such as herself could not possibly be expected to reside in such a place, when Lord Augustus, who had gone into the tavern to make inquiries, returned to say that there were two rooms available, the landlord and his family having agreed to sleep in the stables for the night. The ladies would share one, and he and the coachman, the guard, and Mr Cato would do the best they could with the other.

Hannah was relieved to find that although the inn was very humble indeed, it was spotlessly clean. Mr Cato said that, as Lord Augustus had given up his pin to the adventure, he himself would foot the bill.

They wearily sat down to supper. Now that they were so close, they all felt more hopeless than ever. The landlord and his wife bustled about, laying plates of food, gratified to have so many guests.

'Tell me, landlord,' asked Lord Augustus, 'does Lady Carsey still reside in Esher?'

'That she does, me lord, but saving your noble presence, I'd rather not be talking about the lady.'

'Pray tell me why?'

The landlord looked mutinous and his wife frightened.

Penelope, with a sudden flash of intuition, said loudly, 'We all hate her, you see, and think her a monster.'

The landlord paused and wiped his hands slowly on his apron.

'That be different then, for we're sore angry with my lady. Our eldest, Greta, was in service to my lady and come home this very day, crying fit to die. Seems she broke a vase and my lady summoned her and whipped her. So she run home, all the way. Nothing the likes of I can do, her being so powerful in the town.'

'Could we speak to your Greta?' asked Hannah suddenly. 'You see, she may know news of my footman, Benjamin.' Briefly she told the landlord of Benjamin's adventures at the hands of Lady Carsey.

'I mind that,' said the landlord, amazed. 'It were the talk of the town.' He turned to his wife. 'Fetch our Greta here.'

They waited anxiously until the landlord's wife returned with a young woman whose face was blotched with weeping.

'Now, Greta,' said Hannah in the matter-of-fact voice she had used in the past to quieten frightened servants, 'do you remember Benjamin, the deaf-and-dumb footman?'

Greta nodded.

'We fear Lady Carsey has sent ruffians to capture him. Did you hear anything strange during the night? Last night?'

Greta shook her head and twisted her apron. Hannah sighed and then she had an idea. 'Does Lady Carsey find it hard to keep servants, Greta?'

'Oh, yes, mum. There's a few as 'ave bin with 'er ever so long and right nasty they be. But the housekeeper, she left along o' me. Said she reported the broken vase but didn't say as 'ow I had done it and she would 'ave no truck wi' the whipping of girls.'

'Excellent,' said Hannah. 'You may go, Greta.' She turned to the others, her odd eyes flashing green with excitement. 'I have a plan!'

'I thought you would think of something before long,' murmured Lord Augustus. 'Go on, Miss Pym the Redoubtable, and tell us all.'

'It is but seven in the evening,' said Hannah. 'I can still go to the Manor directly and apply for the post of housekeeper.'

'And what good will that do?' asked Miss Trenton sourly.

'Let me see,' said Hannah, ignoring her. 'Mr Cato can drive me there, if the innkeeper has some sort of gig or cart. If I get the job, he will return for you, Lord Augustus. You and Mr Cato will hide in the grounds. If I have found Benjamin, I will light a candle and wave it across one of the front windows.'

Lord Augustus raised his quizzing-glass and surveyed Hannah's expensive gown of fine kerseymere wool. 'And how do you expect to get away with it, Miss Pym? Lady Carsey has already met you.'

'She did not really look at me,' said Hannah, 'nor did her butler. I was a bore in her eyes. She looked at Miss Wilkins because she was jealous of her and she looked at you, my lord, most of the time.'

'But will she take you for a servant, Miss Pym? Your clothes will give you away.'

Hannah coloured and gave a tug at her crooked nose. She had her housekeeper's gown in her trunk. Sir George Clarence had deposited Hannah's legacy in the bank for her, but Hannah still did not trust banks and feared to learn that the bankers had run off with her money and so she had kept her servant's dress just in case she ever needed it again.

'I have something that will do,' she said, avoiding Miss Trenton's eyes, which were uncomfortably sharp.

'Well, what do you think?' Lord Augustus asked Mr Cato when Hannah had gone upstairs to change.

Mr Cato shook his head. 'Now that we're all here and going into action as it were, I'm beginning to think we've all run mad. What if one of the waiters at the inn thought Benjamin had money and attacked him, knowing that a deaf-and-dumb man could not cry out? It may have nothing to do with Lady Carsey.'

'We're here, and we may as well go through with it,' said Penelope. 'I will accompany you to the grounds and wait for Miss Pym's signal.'

'No!' said both men at once.

'But that is not fair! You are prepared to let her go alone into the house of that creature and yet you will not even let me go as far as the grounds where I may be able to be of some support to Miss Pym should harm befall her.' Lord Augustus thought indulgently that Penelope looked like an infuriated kitten.

'We'll see,' he said, and Penelope had to be content with that.

Hannah reappeared and the company surveyed her in surprise. She was wearing a severe gown of black bombazine and an awesome cap. So our Miss Pym *has* been a housekeeper, thought Lord Augustus, and Miss Trenton said acidly, 'Why, Miss Pym, you are the veriest servant. One would think you had been one all your life.'

Lord Augustus went out to find the landlord and returned to say that he had a horse and cart available for their use.

Everyone was highly excited now that the adventure was underway, except Miss Trenton, who sat a little away from the others, looking strangely wistful.

As the cart bearing Hannah and Mr Cato jogged off into the night, the others returned to the inn to wait.

Penelope searched through her luggage until she found a plain dark dress she had worn for writing classes, dark so that ink-stains would not show. It had expensive lace at the collar and cuffs, which she carefully cut off. She found a cap, one of the frivolous kind meant to be worn under a bonnet, and took the lace edging off that before tying it on her head.

Lord Augustus was not impressed. 'If, by any mad folly, we do take you with us,' he said, 'that white cap will show in the darkness.' Penelope took it off and threw it down on a chair. 'Then I shall go without it,' she said defiantly. 'I do wonder what Miss Pym is doing. It's a mercy Lady Carsey really saw only you, my lord.' Then she reflected under what circumstances Lord Augustus had seen Lady Carsey and of how much he had probably seen of that lady, and she blushed fiery-red in the candlelight. Lord Augustus looked at that blush and reflected with a tinge of regret that Miss Trenton had made up that story about Penelope. The girl positively screamed Virgin.

Hannah felt nervous and strung up as Mr Cato drove up the Manor drive. 'To the kitchen door,' whispered Hannah urgently, seeing the American was about to stop at the front. 'It will be at the far side. No, leave me here and I will find it on foot.'

'But what if they won't have you?' protested Mr Cato. 'You don't want to have to walk back.'

'Then wait on the road outside the grounds. If I am not with you in half an hour, say, then go and fetch Lord Augustus.'

Mr Cato watched Hannah's spare figure as she

resolutely marched to the side of the building. She had her trunk in her hand. He found himself admiring her tremendously. Hannah Pym, he thought, would make a good American.

Hannah found the servants' entrance and raised her hand and knocked loudly at the door.

While she waited, she thought herself into her role. She was desperately in need of work. She had been travelling through Esher to stay with relatives in Portsmouth and had learned that the Manor was in need of a housekeeper. She was once more Hannah Pym, servant.

After some time had passed and she was just raising her hand to knock again, she heard the shuffle of footsteps. The door swung open. The butler she had seen before, holding a candle in a flat stick, surveyed her. He was a cadaverous-looking man in his shirt-sleeves and wearing a baize apron.

'I heard there was a vacancy for a housekeeper, and I am come to apply for the post,' said Hannah firmly.

'At this time of night!'

'What better time,' said Hannah briskly. 'Are you going to keep me on this doorstep, sir, or are you going to ask me inside?'

The butler reluctantly stood aside. Hannah walked through a scullery into a large shadowy kitchen that smelt strongly of onions and grease. After the kitchen came the servants' hall. The servants were just finishing their supper. Hannah thought that, apart from a few frightened girls, she had never seen such a villainous crew.

'This here,' announced the butler behind her, 'is some female who wants the housekeeper's job. What's your name?'

'Miss Hannah Pym,' said Hannah firmly, seeing no reason to lie about her name. On that visit to the Manor, only Lord Augustus had presented his card.

'Wait here and I'll tell mistress.' The butler shrugged himself into his coat after removing his apron and shambled out. Hannah sat down at the table with the others, who surveyed her in silence.

'Are you not going to offer me some refreshment?' snapped Hannah.

The servants looked at each other, and then one of the footmen rose, took a tankard from the shelf, and filled it with house ale from a barrel and then set it down in front of her with a bang.

Hannah raised her tankard. 'The King!' she said.

The others echoed the toast.

Silence fell again. Hannah could feel herself becoming increasingly nervous.

By the time the butler returned to say that my lady would see her, Hannah felt she had been sitting there a lifetime. She picked up her trunk, determined not to leave it behind in the servants' hall in case anyone looked inside it, and with the heavy bag banging against her legs, she followed the butler up the stairs. She left her trunk in the hall, hoping it would be safe there. The butler led the way up to a drawing-room on the first floor and threw open the doors.

'Here is the person who has come about the job,' he said.

Hannah gave a quick tug to her cap so that the frill fell lower over her forehead, shadowing her face.

She walked into the room and stood with her hands clasped in front of her and her eyes lowered.

'Name?' demanded Lady Carsey.

'Miss Hannah Pym.'

'Ah, so my butler said. Why "miss"?'

'I never adopted the courtesy title of "Mrs",' said Hannah.

'Experience?'

Hannah raised her eyes briefly and then lowered them again quickly. There was something uncomfortably sharp and penetrating about Lady Carsey's gaze.

'I was only with one household, my lady. Mr Clarence of Thornton Hall, Kensington. He died a few months ago. I started in a lowly position in that household and rose to the position of housekeeper. I keep excellent and correct accounts. I am expert at training maids. I work hard.'

Lady Carsey held out her hand. 'References?'

Hannah opened her reticule and slowly took out a stiff folded piece of paper. When she had been sure that Mr Clarence was dying, she had asked him for a reference. She reluctantly handed it to Lady Carsey, for she was afraid she would not get it back.

Lady Carsey who, it seemed, did not trouble about her appearance in front of servants, popped a serviceable pair of glasses on her nose and read. 'Dear me,' she murmured, 'Mr Clarence makes you sound the veriest paragon. But what is such a paragon doing on my doorstep at this hour of the night?'

'I was travelling to stay with relatives in Portsmouth,' said Hannah, 'and heard there was a vacancy here. I have used up my savings. It seemed a good opportunity.'

Lady Carsey leaned back in her chair and swung one slippered foot. She waved the precious reference to and fro, perilously near the flame of a candle.

'I demand absolute loyalty from my servants,' she said. 'I will not tolerate gossiping in the town. You will be allowed two days off a year and your salary will be eighteen pounds a year, to be paid out on quarter-day. You are on trial. Biggs, the butler, will report to me of how you go on. I will not tolerate insolence in my servants. Do I make myself clear?'

'Yes, my lady.'

Lady Carsey rang the bell. When the butler appeared, she said, 'Biggs, show Miss Pym to her room and explain her duties. She is on trial. Watch her carefully.' She waved a white hand to show the interview was at an end. She had not even bothered to ask Hannah whether she wanted the job or whether she considered the terms favourable.

Hannah gave a low curtsy and then held out her hand. 'My reference, my lady.'

'No, I shall keep this,' said Lady Carsey. 'It will need to be checked.'

Hannah stifled an exclamation of dismay. If she found Benjamin, she would have no time to waste looking for that reference.

She followed the butler out. She picked up her trunk in the hall and said, 'Show me to my quarters.'

'You will address me as Mr Biggs at all times,' said the butler heavily. 'Don't go getting uppity with me. Better be pleasant, too. I can get my lady to send you packing any time I want.'

He suddenly leered at Hannah, who gave him a slow smile and fluttered her short sandy eyelashes. The servants who had once been under her command would have been amazed to see the stern Miss Pym trying to flirt.

The housekeeper's room was on a half-landing on the back staircase. The butler followed her in. 'I shall just prettify myself, Mr Biggs,' said Hannah with a coy titter, 'and then I will join you in the servants' hall.'

The butler grinned, pinched Hannah's bony bottom, and shuffled out.

'I shall slap his face before this night is out,' muttered Hannah. She opened her trunk and took out a length of stout cord and then fastened it to the handle. She opened the window, noticing with relief that it overlooked the front, and lowered the trunk down into the bushes. Then, squaring her shoulders, she went down to the servants' hall.

Her heart sank when she pushed open the door. Mr Biggs was alone. She guessed he had sent all the other servants off to bed so as to indulge in a little dalliance with the new housekeeper.

'A little brandy, Miss Pym,' said Biggs.

'Yes, I thank you,' said Hannah. 'But first, may I have my keys and a tour of the house? I am anxious to begin my work early.'

Biggs scowled, but he could not risk Lady Carsey's

finding a housekeeper in the morning who did not know where anything was.

Hannah followed him around the house, or rather tried always to keep behind him, for if she moved in front, he pinched her bottom. If I really were going to be housekeeper here, thought Hannah, noticing dirty hearths and cobwebs, I would make some changes. Although she appeared to listen intently, she had no interest in which keys fitted which doors on the upper storeys. Back downstairs she insisted on examining the still-room. 'Why do you not have a brandy yourself until I examine all these bottles,' said Hannah. 'What if my lady should want, say, rose-water?'

'Don't be all night about it,' growled the butler, but he retreated to the servants' hall. Hannah's sharp eyes ranged over the bottles. She took down a little bottle of laudanum and put it in her pocket. Then, fastening the keys firmly at her waist, she went into the servants' hall. 'You have not shown me the cellars,' she said.

Biggs stiffened. 'That's my preserve,' he said suspiciously. 'What was you wanting to see the cellars for?'

'Because, my dear Mr Biggs, should you fall ill, I would need to know which wines were which and in which bins to find them.'

'Sit down. I'm never ill. Tell you what, two days' time and I'll take you down. Finished then.'

'Finished with what?' demanded Hannah.

'Finished cleaning them cellars.'

'Oh.' Hannah sat down at the table and looked into his eyes and smiled. 'What about that brandy, Mr Biggs?'

'Give us a kiss first.'

'Oh, Mr Biggs,' said Hannah coyly. 'You are the veriest rake. One little drink to give me courage.'

He grinned and poured a glass for her and refilled his own.

'What's that?' cried Hannah suddenly, pointing over to a door that she was sure led to the cellars.

The butler started up with an oath, tipping his chair over, and ran to the low door. He pressed his ear against it and listened hard. Hannah took out the bottle of laudanum and tipped a generous measure into the butler's glass.

'Nothing there,' he said, coming back and sitting down. 'Rats, most like.'

Hannah gave a feminine shudder. 'La! I do so detest rats.' She raised her glass. 'To you, Mr Biggs.'

He drained his glass in one gulp. 'Now,' he said, edging his chair next to her own, 'what about that kiss?'

Hannah screwed her eyes up and puckered up her mouth. She would just have to endure it. His mouth approached her own and she shuddered as brandy fumes fanned her face. Then his lips descended on hers. Hannah's stomach heaved with revulsion. She thought she could not bear it a moment longer and was just about to push him away when his mouth became slack and then slid wetly from her own. He looked at her in a fuddled way and then put a shaky hand to his brow.

'I hope my kiss has not made you faint, sir,' said Hannah archly.

He tugged at his cravat. 'It's hot in here,' he said faintly. His dimming eyes looked at the glass and then at Hannah. 'Why, you bitch,' he said thickly. His hands reached out for her throat. Hannah darted from her chair and stood with her back to the wall. He heaved himself up and came at her. She darted away to the far side of the room. He stumbled towards her and then with a groan fell headlong on the floor. Soon he was breathing deeply, completely unconscious.

Hannah found she was trembling. She thought of Sir George Clarence and wished he were there. She felt very weak and womanly.

'Courage,' she told herself aloud.

She went to the cellar door, or the door she was sure led to the cellars. Then she realized the folly of not paying attention to which key fitted which lock. She would now have to try them all. But first she went back to the door of the servants' hall and patiently tried all the keys until she found the right one and locked herself in. Now for that cellar.

It was a very large keyhole, so she tried all the large keys until at last she found the right one. The door swung open. Hannah picked up a candle and made her way down. The cellar was cool and musty. She walked between the high racks of wine. It was no use calling to Benjamin. He could not hear her or shout a reply.

After half an hour of diligent searching, she sat wearily down on a wine barrel. There was no sign of the footman.

She sat and prayed for help. She could not think what else to do.

Then suddenly a thought came into her head. If Benjamin had still been unconscious when he was brought to the Manor, he would have been dragged to whatever prison they had ready for him.

She rose and picked up the candle and went back to the foot of the stairs and began to study the floor. And then she saw them – two trails across the dusty floor, looking like the marks made by heels when a body was dragged across the ground.

She followed the marks, which stopped at a wine barrel set on the floor. She looked around the barrel, but there were no more marks. She raised the lid of the barrel. It was full of wine. Shaking a little with fear, she rolled up her sleeve and plunged an arm down into the wine in case Benjamin had been drowned like the poor Duke of Clarence. She could feel nothing. Perhaps there was something under the barrel. A trapdoor.

She set down the candle in its flat stick and tried to move the barrel but could not.

She looked around the cellar until she found a small firkin. Using it as a pail, she began to bail out the wine, spilling it on the cellar floor, working with such haste that her dress became soaked in wine.

At last, she seized the barrel by the rim and heaved, and with a loud scraping noise she was able to move it to one side.

And there, below it, was a trapdoor. It was not bolted or padlocked. Hannah opened it. A flight of wooden steps led downward. Again she retrieved the candle and down she went, turning at the bottom of the stairs and holding the candle high.

Benjamin lay in a corner of a small cell-like dungeon. His face was white and his eyes were closed. His wrists and ankles were bound. There was blood on his forehead and his livery was dusty and torn.

Hannah crouched down beside him and shook his shoulder gently. To her immeasurable relief, his eyes opened. The look of sheer gratitude and gladness in them brought a lump to Hannah's throat.

'Now, then, Benjamin,' she whispered, 'watch my lips. I have a small pair of nail-scissors in my pocket. If they will not sever your bonds, I shall have to risk returning to the kitchen for a knife.'

Hannah worked at the thick rope that bound him but the fragile nail-scissors snapped. 'Wait here,' she said.

Now in an agony of fear and impatience, Hannah climbed back up through the cellar and up to the kitchen. She found a sharp carving knife and made her way down again.

Quickly she sawed through his bonds. She helped him to his feet. His face was screwed up with pain and she could only guess that it was caused by the circulation returning to his feet and hands.

She hitched one of his arms about her shoulders and together they staggered to the staircase. Hannah blew out the candle and then pushed Benjamin in front of her and he began to climb the wooden stairs, slowly and stiffly.

When they both reached the cellar, Hannah took a deep breath. Taking the footman's hand, she guided him through the blackness to the cellar stairs and then led him upwards.

Benjamin tripped over the body of the butler and fell headlong with a crash. Hannah helped him up and thrust him into a chair. She lit an oil lamp on the table.

'Now, try to understand,' said Hannah earnestly. Benjamin watched her lips closely. 'The others will be in the grounds. I must go up to one of the windows and wave a candle as signal to them to bring the cart to the front door. I am going to lock you in here for safety.' Benjamin nodded and then seized her hand and raised it to his lips.

'No time for that,' said Hannah, snatching her hand away. She unlocked the door of the servants' hall and then locked it again behind her, praying that no one in the household would awake.

'Well, you would come,' said Lord Augustus crossly. Penelope shivered and rain dripped from her small nose. A thin drizzle had started to fall. They were hidden in the bushes. Mr Cato with the horse and cart had been left outside the gate. Lord Augustus had arranged with him that as soon as he saw that light at the window, he would hoot like an owl. But it turned out to be a busy night for owls, and several times the horse and cart had come charging up the drive. Penelope at last said she would run and fetch Mr Cato as soon as they saw that candle.

'What can be keeping her?' asked Penelope. 'All the lights in the house seem to have been out for hours.'

'The simple explanation, my sweet,' said Lord

Augustus, stifling a yawn, 'is that we were mistaken and Benjamin is not there. It was but a thin chance. And now I have given away my pin. It was quite my favourite. Do you not think it became me?'

'I think it is very unmanly in you to worry about your appearance when poor Benjamin could be in some dark dungeon.'

'It is not the custom for manor-houses, however ancient, to have dungeons. It is hardly a medieval stronghold. And if you twit me about my manliness, I shall kiss you.'

'Faugh! How can you flirt at a time like this?'

They were both crouched down in the bushes. He could just make out the white glimmer of her face. He put a firm hand under her chin and bent his lips and kissed her full on the mouth.

Shocked, Penelope went very still. It was like music, thought Lord Augustus dreamily – fast, turbulent music with one sweet chord piercing through it all. Her lips were soft and warm and yielding. He could kiss her all night. He could kiss her for the rest of her life. She wore a light flowery perfume, seductive to his senses. At last he freed his lips and looked at her in a dazed way.

'I suppose you kissed Lady Carsey like that,' said Penelope in a choked little voice.

'Damn you,' he said fiercely. 'I have never kissed anyone like that in my life before.'

'And you have kissed many,' said Penelope, her temper rising.

Candlelight flickered frantically back and forth at

one of the front windows, but the angry couple did not notice.

Hannah put down the candlestick and stared out. There was no sign of anyone. Surely the cart should be rumbling up the short drive. She thought she heard a faint sound upstairs in the house and seized the candle again and waved it frantically. In her fear and agitation, she did not notice that one of the inner lace curtains that she had pulled to one side had caught alight. She kept on waving the candle until there was a sudden sheet of flame as the curtain went up. Hannah dropped the lighted candle in a panic on the floor and ran down to the servants' hall, fumbling with the keys in a paroxysm of terror until she found the right one.

Mr Cato from his post on the road saw the sheet of flame, swore, and called to his horse. He shouted, 'My lord,' at the top of his voice as the cart charged up the drive.

Lord Augustus and Penelope erupted from the bushes and stared in consternation at the flames at the window.

'Faith!' exclaimed Lord Augustus. 'I think she has run mad and set the house alight.'

Upstairs in the Manor, Lady Carsey awoke and sat up. She had been dreaming about Lord Augustus. She cursed the trickster under her breath. And then, all at once, she remembered when she had first met him, how he had called with the pretty chit and that severe-looking female with the odd eyes.

Odd eyes.

Her own eyes widened. She had seen those eyes, and only recently.

The housekeeper.

With an oath, she seized the bell-rope beside the bed and began to ring it furiously.

Her lady's maid came running in. 'Fetch Biggs. Get all the men,' snapped Lady Carsey. 'The new housekeeper is a spy. Make sure she does not escape.'

The lady's maid gave a terrified squawk and ran from the room, only to return a moment later, her eyes dilated. 'The house is on fire, my lady. It's burning bad.'

Lord Augustus, clutching Penelope, watched the fire take hold. And then he saw Hannah leading Benjamin around the side of the house. 'In the cart,' he called.

Benjamin was bundled into the cart, with Hannah after him.

'We cannot leave,' moaned Penelope. 'We cannot leave them all to die in the flames.'

And then round the side of the house, from the servants' entrance, came the staff, led by Lady Carsey. 'They've all got out by the back stairs,' shouted Lord Augustus, just as Lady Carsey saw them. He thrust Penelope in the cart and jumped up after her as Mr Cato urged the cart and horse down the drive, whipping the horse into a gallop.

They hung grimly on to the sides as the old cart bucked along the rutted roads.

Finally Mr Cato slowed the horse to a canter. 'Got

clear,' he said. 'Was it you, Miss Pym, who set the place alight?'

'I did not mean to,' said Hannah, trembling with shock. 'I waved the candle and waved the candle but could not see a sign of anyone. I tried again and that must have been when I set the curtains alight. Oh, she will have all the police and all the justices in the land after me.'

'Calm yourself,' said Lord Augustus. 'She will not dare. We have Benjamin, and although Benjamin cannot speak, we know he can write. He can testify that he was taken away by force and imprisoned. She cannot risk that.'

Hannah heaved a sigh of relief, then her face clouded. 'My good trunk. I left it behind.'

'Were all your clothes in it?' asked Penelope.

'No, only rocks to weigh it down. But it was a good and faithful trunk. I have also lost my . . .'

'What?' demanded Mr Cato over his shoulder.

'Nothing,' said Hannah. She had been about to say, 'I have also lost my precious reference,' but only Penelope knew Hannah had been a servant and she did not want any of the others to know.

Instead she said, 'Why did you not see the candle the first time I waved it, Lord Augustus?'

'I must have fallen asleep,' he said blandly.

'Miss Wilkins?'

'I was so dreadfully tired, I must have dropped asleep as well,' said Penelope in a low voice.

'Well, I think we have had our revenge on Lady Carsey,' said Lord Augustus. 'We shall not be hearing from her again. But I am afraid there is no rest for us this night. We must rouse Miss Trenton and the coachman and be on our way. We shall swear the landlord to secrecy. He will no doubt be delighted to hear what you have done, Miss Pym.'

5

One road leads to London,
One road runs to Wales,
My road leads me seawards
To the white dipping sails.

John Masefield

Miss Trenton did not sleep. She found she could not. She longed to hear the return of the others, to learn that the footman had not been found, and it had all been for nothing. That way, she could comfort herself with doing the right thing by not getting involved in such a hare-brained adventure.

Many harsh things had been said to Miss Trenton in the past, but none had struck home like the remark made to her by Mr Cato: that it was her lack of adventure which had kept her a maid.

It was not true, she kept telling herself. What absolute folly, to expect her, a gentlewoman, to embark on such a ploy to rescue a mere footman, and perhaps get arrested herself in doing so. Such was not an adventure but pure stupidity. A little voice in her head kept nagging at her that no one had expected her to go, but she tried not to listen to it.

Then she heard the rumble of the cart arriving. She was still fully dressed, so she made her way downstairs in time to join the landlord, his wife, the coachman, and guard, who appeared to have been waiting as anxiously as she had been herself, but for different reasons.

The landlord lit the lamps in the low-raftered tap and stirred up the fire.

The inn door opened and the first thing Miss Trenton saw with a sinking heart was the bloodied Benjamin, supported by Mr Cato and Lord Augustus. All, with the exception of Miss Trenton, demanded to know what had happened. Benjamin was tenderly placed in front of the fire and given brandy. Hannah and Penelope entered, fully recovered from their fright, their eyes shining with excitement. Lord Augustus told of the fire and Hannah of finding Benjamin in the undercellar.

There was a sour taste like bile in Miss Trenton's mouth. She could not possibly imagine herself bailing out a barrel of wine, or of creeping about in the dark.

She affected to be horrified. 'But we shall all be arrested!' she cried. 'Setting poor Lady Carsey's house on fire.'

Mr Cato looked at her with contempt as they all took their places round the fire.

'Calm yourself,' said Lord Augustus. 'She would not dare. Miss Pym, find your notebook and let us see if Benjamin is strong enough to write his adventures.'

Hannah did as she was told and as Benjamin wrote busily, the landlord said, 'No one shall hear a thing from me. You have my word on it. But they will be looking for you.'

'Yes, we must leave soon,' said Hannah. 'Be so good as to pack, Miss Trenton.'

'I had not unpacked,' said Miss Trenton.

'Beats all,' said the coachman, his eyes round with wonder. 'Best adventure I ever did hear. Like a book, it is. I'll be getting the coach ready and we'll be off as soon as we can.'

Hannah took the notebook from Benjamin and said, 'He says he remembers being struck on the head at the inn and the next thing he knew he was lying on the floor of the carriage. He tried to struggle up and they struck him again. He regained consciousness in the prison in which I found him. He has had nothing to eat or drink.'

'I'll prepare something for the poor man to eat in the carriage,' said the landlord.

'Benjamin's head needs bathing,' exclaimed Penelope. 'Can you also bring me a basin of warm water and a flannel?'

'We should really shave his head and put a plaster of vinegar and brown paper on that nasty bump,' said Mr Cato.

'Haven't time for that,' retorted Hannah briskly.

'We can rest as soon as we reach an inn as far away from here as possible. Lady Carsey may have sent her servants to look for us. She saw us in the light of the fire.'

Lord Augustus thought for a few moments. 'No, I do not think she will want us found. There is Benjamin to explain away, you see.'

'Then now that you have this . . . this servant,' said Miss Trenton angrily, 'why do you not take him to the nearest magistrate so that Lady Carsey may be arrested?'

'Because we would all be held in Esher during the lengthy inquiries,' pointed out Lord Augustus. 'Besides, the magistrate favours Lady Carsey, and, although finding her guilty, may bring a separate charge against Miss Pym. It could be proved, you know, that Miss Pym had deliberately masqueraded as a servant for the sole purpose of setting the house alight. The jury would be composed of local people, and juries have been bribed or frightened by such as Lady Carsey before. I think we are all well out of it. But, just in case, I think we should leave.'

'You are an excellent woman, Miss Pym!' cried Mr Cato suddenly. 'What say you to an offer to sail with me to America as my wife?'

There was a startled silence.

A small glow of gratification spread through Hannah Pym's thin body. She did not want to marry Mr Cato, but how wonderful to get a proposal of marriage.

'Sir, I am most honoured,' said Hannah, 'but I fear

I am too used to my single state to want to change it now.'

'Think on it,' said Mr Cato cheerfully. 'We should deal excellent well together.'

Now Miss Trenton's fury knew no bounds. She could just about bear Lord Augustus's attentions to the beautiful Penelope. But the plain-featured Miss Pym getting a proposal of marriage! It was too much. She felt quite tearful and weak after the spasm of rage passed.

'I shall collect my belongings,' she said shakily. No one seemed to take any notice of her leaving. Penelope was tenderly bathing Benjamin's head and Lord Augustus was watching her. Mr Cato was beaming at Hannah and the coachman and guard were surveying them all in open-mouthed admiration.

Soon they were all back in the coach, Hannah having had to buy a fusty old trunk from the landlord in which to put her clothes. She sat making calculations as the coach lurched through the night. She would need to buy another suit of livery for Benjamin, and a new trunk.

Penelope yawned and shivered. She had not bothered to change her wet clothes. Her hair lay in damp tendrils against her cheek. She could not stop thinking about Lord Augustus and that kiss, the first she had ever received. It had been sweetness itself, but he was an experienced man and was probably expert at seducing women. She looked up at him and he gave her a lazy smile and she blushed and looked away. Soon her eyelids began to droop and she fell asleep, her head finally coming to rest on his shoulder. Lord

Augustus put an arm about her to cradle her against him and finally fell asleep himself.

Lady Carsey was once more in bed. The fire engine had arrived quickly and only a small morning-room on the first floor had been gutted. The rest of the house was intact. She had been very lucky. The pale light of dawn was filtering through the curtains. She had been awake a long time, fearing any moment the arrival of the police. But it began to occur to her that those wretched fiends of the stage-coach planned to leave her alone. Relief that there was to be no retribution was quickly followed by a choking rage and a desire for revenge. Her hatred this time was not focused on Lord Augustus but on Miss Hannah Pym. That creature had had the temerity to use her own name, as that reference had proved. No one ever crossed Lady Carsey and got away with it! She lay awake a long time, making plans.

The weary coachman drew up at the Anchor in Liphook. Penelope awoke to find her head resting on Lord Augustus's chest, and, what was worse, one of her hands resting on that gentleman's thigh. She drew away from him as if scorched.

As the passengers alighted, Miss Trenton fell into step beside Lord Augustus. 'Did you mark how wantonly she lay against you?' she hissed. 'Surely that bears out what I have told you?'

He looked down at her under drooping eyelids and then said clearly and precisely, 'You are an unlovely

101

woman, Miss Trenton, because you have a carping, mean, and unlovely soul,' and then he strode before her into the inn. Miss Trenton stood stock-still and burst into tears, but it was a lachrymose age when everyone prided themselves on their ability to cry, and so no one even turned around to inquire why she was so distressed.

The passengers were weary, but on the coachman's reminding them that they were now only twenty-six miles from Portsmouth, all agreed to dine and go on. Benjamin wrote that he felt well enough to stand the rest of the journey.

They dined quickly and then returned to the coach. Now no one was asleep, except Benjamin. Hannah fretted that the journey's end was near and she saw little hope of making a match between Penelope and Lord Augustus. Miss Trenton was worrying whether her friend would be able to give her a job. Mr Cato was regretting the adventure; the time taken on it probably did mean he would need to wait in Portsmouth for another ship. Penelope was beginning to dread her father's disappointment. Lord Augustus drearily contemplated a boring stay with his uncle and would not admit to himself that Penelope's comparing him to a vulture waiting for the old man to die had anything to do with his sudden distaste for the scheme.

The coach finally creaked and rumbled into the yard at the George in Portsmouth. Hannah scrubbed at the steamy glass of the window with her handkerchief to see if she could see the sea, but there was only the light and bustle of the inn yard.

Miss Trenton and Mr Cato said they would put up for the night at the inn, as did Hannah. Hannah wanted to spend some time in Portsmouth, buy Benjamin a new livery and get a physician to examine the wound on his head. Lord Augustus said he would stay at the inn as well. It was too late to rouse his uncle.

Penelope felt lost. Her father, she knew, would have been watching and waiting for news of the Portsmouth coach. He was no doubt waiting for her inside the inn. She would go back to her old cosseted and isolated life and probably, she thought miserably, no more adventures would happen to her ever again.

And as she walked towards the inn, there was her father, small and squat, wearing a tie-wig slightly askew over his weather-beaten face. She ran straight into his outstretched arms, babbling she was so very sorry about the seminary, but that it wasn't her fault, and she had had such adventures, and a tumbled tale of Benjamin and Lady Carsey fell on the bewildered chandler's ears.

'Here now, chuck,' said Mr Wilkins. 'Let us go into the inn and take a dish of tea and you shall tell me all, for your mother is sore disappointed in you.' Which Penelope, through experience, took to mean that *he* was disappointed, for her mother, she knew, never voiced an opinion on anything.

'Pray, Papa,' said Penelope, 'would you please ask the other passengers to dine with us? They will help me explain what happened.'

Glad to have his daughter safe, Mr Wilkins readily

agreed. By general consent, although Miss Trenton could be heard to sniff loudly, Benjamin was allowed to sit down with them.

Mr Wilkins took the head of the table. He had been introduced to all, and was excited that his Penelope had been having her adventures in the company of a personable young lord. Penelope's disgrace at the seminary was quite driven out of his mind.

He listened enraptured to the tale of their exploits, his eyes occasionally studying Lord Augustus hopefully, but that young man was lounging at his ease and not once had he even glanced in Penelope's direction.

Miss Trenton, for once, toyed with her food. She could not believe that Penelope was going to get off scot-free. After all the adventures in which Miss Trenton did not feature were repeated over again to the admiring Mr Wilkins, she coughed genteelly and said, 'I am sure you are delighted to have your daughter safe with you, Mr Wilkins, and will forgive her for her dreadful behaviour at the seminary.'

'What's this?' demanded Mr Wilkins fiercely. 'I got a letter from that Miss Jasper saying as how some master had become spoony over my Penelope. I was angry at first, but just look at her, my lord. Ain't she enough to turn any man's head?'

'Indeed, she is,' drawled Lord Augustus. His blue eyes turned on Miss Trenton. 'Although I must say that I was extremely shocked by Miss Trenton's disclosure that the music master had only proposed to Miss Wilkins because he felt, having ruined her, that it was the best he could do.'

There was an appalled silence. Miss Trenton turned quite white.

'And how did you come by this information, ma'am?' asked Mr Wilkins awfully.

Miss Trenton gave a little choking sound.

'I will tell you,' said Hannah Pym furiously. 'I will tell you, Mr Wilkins, how it came about. Miss Trenton, because of sour jealousy, made the whole thing up. Is that not so, Miss Trenton?'

'Lord Augustus is mistaken,' said Miss Trenton. 'I said no such thing!'

'Are you calling me a liar?' demanded Lord Augustus maliciously.

Miss Trenton shot to her feet. 'You are all horrible. All of you,' she screamed. 'I *hate* you all!'

And with that, she ran from the room.

'There you have it,' said Lord Augustus languidly. 'The explanation for your daughter's disgrace at the seminary and silly Miss Trenton's remarks is quite simple, Mr Wilkins. Her appearance not only excites admiration but jealousy. I gather she has been kept much at home. Surely there are balls and assemblies she could attend in Portsmouth and young people of her own age she could meet? She is much to be pitied.'

'I'll have none o' that,' retorted Mr Wilkins. 'She's had the best of everything.'

'In material terms, yes,' agreed Lord Augustus.

Mr Wilkins bit back the angry reply he had been about to make. He had no desire to quarrel with a man he was already marking out as his future son-in-law.

Instead he said with a forced laugh, 'I must be taking my puss home. Here is my address, my lord.' He handed over his card. 'You will no doubt be calling.'

Hannah waited hopefully.

'I am afraid not,' said Lord Augustus. 'I shall be much occupied while I am here.'

Penelope felt exactly as if he had slapped her. All her fears about that kiss were true. He had only been amusing himself.

'Coming, Papa,' she said meekly. 'Papa, do give Miss Pym a card and tell her to call, for she has been kindness itself.'

'Gladly,' said Mr Wilkins, taking out his card-case again.

Hannah hated to see Penelope leave. She felt they had all become a sort of ill-assorted family, and now the family was breaking up, with no happy ending for anyone but Benjamin.

After Penelope and her father had left, Hannah sent Benjamin up to bed, telling him to stay there in the morning until she had found the services of a doctor to attend him. Mr Cato yawned and remarked he was devilish tired and took himself off. Hannah was left alone with Lord Augustus.

'I do not know how you do it, Miss Pym,' said Lord Augustus admiringly. 'I am nigh dead with fatigue, and yet you look bright as a button.'

'I cannot help thinking you might have found time, my lord, to call on Mr Wilkins.'

'You mean Mr Wilkins's daughter. She is a very

pretty little girl, Miss Pym. What more would you have?'

He looked down his nose at her, his eyes cold, as if defying her to suggest he should even contemplate paying court to the daughter of a chandler.

Hannah had, of course, been just about to pursue that matter further. But she abruptly changed tack.

'I did expect you might want to call,' she said, 'and it was quite silly of me. Despite Mr Wilkins's ambitions, I really cannot see him in the end throwing his daughter away on a penniless lord. I thought he seemed a man of good sense.'

'So you do not think I am a prize in any way?' mocked Lord Augustus.

'Of course not,' said Hannah comfortably. 'Be so good as to ring the bell and ask the landlord to fetch tea, I do enjoy a dish of bohea before bedtime.'

He gave her a slightly baffled look. Mr Wilkins had been so obviously hopeful of a match between Lord Augustus and his daughter that it had thrown cold water on that young man's affections. Penniless he might be, but Lord Augustus knew he was considered a catch. He was used to being pursued. He had great contempt for his friends who had stooped to marry rich merchants' daughters for their dowries. Penelope Wilkins was worth more, so much more, than some fortune-hunting adventurer.

After Hannah had been served tea, she looked across the table at him. Her eyes turned blue and seemed, for such as Hannah Pym, to look unusually innocent.

107

'I shall call,' said Hannah, 'for as you rightly accused me, I am a determined matchmaker. Penelope Wilkins is likely to fall for the first eligible man, and that will never do. I am determined to persuade her parents to take her to balls and assemblies. She will become accustomed to masculine admiration and will learn how to discriminate between the genuine and the false. With her strict upbringing, a man who marries her for her money and then neglects her after marriage will not do. She needs a lover as well as a husband. Someone who will take her in his arms and cherish her.'

The picture of Penelope in someone else's arms was suddenly appalling to Lord Augustus. He glared at Hannah. He was sure she had meant to have just that effect with her words.

'And you have much to do yourself, my lord,' Hannah went on. 'There is, after all, your uncle to be courted for his money-bags.'

'Look here, Miss Pym. We have been through a lot together. I am reluctant to call you impertinent.'

'I apologize most sincerely,' said Hannah meekly. 'And now I must see to Benjamin.'

She rose and left Lord Augustus to his uncomfortable thoughts. Those thoughts turned towards his uncle. His uncle was his mother's brother. He was a retired admiral called Lord James Abernethy and lived in seclusion in Portsmouth. Lord Augustus had last seen him some ten years before. That ten years was a very long time. He could hardly shake the old man by the hand and say, 'If you cannot give me any money now, could you leave me some in your will?'

His conscience gave a sharp, nasty jab and he blamed Hannah Pym bitterly for its awakening. In the clubs of London, waiting for relatives to die was a well-known occupation, or rather preoccupation. I wonder what it is like to be old and realize at last that one has not long to live by the visits of relatives one has not seen in years, he reflected.

The money he had won from Mr Cato would soon be gone. He had a small allowance annually from a trust fund, and his next payment was not due for another two months. He would need to find a pawnshop and pop some piece of jewellery.

He wondered what it would be like if he paid a call on the old boy and tried to entertain him and then just left without asking for anything. He felt a certain lightening of his spirit. Dammit, he thought, I *won't* ask Uncle for anything. I'll see if he can put me up for a few days, that's all. And it would be only civil to call on Mr Wilkins. After all, he had paid for dinner.

Hannah swung open her casement window in the morning, prepared for her first sight of the ocean – and looked straight into the windows of the buildings opposite. But there were sea-gulls wheeling about and her nostrils twitched as she smelled tar and fish and salt.

But before she went exploring, Benjamin had to be attended to. The inn manager, already appealed to the previous evening, told her the physician would be along to attend to Benjamin within the hour. When Hannah went down to the coffee room, Mr Cato was just entering the inn. 'Ship sailed yesterday,' he said as soon as he saw Hannah. 'My fault really. It doesn't do to cut these things too fine. I'll be here for another three weeks at least. What are your plans, Miss Pym?'

'I have to wait and see that Benjamin is well enough to get up,' said Hannah. 'Then I must go out and find him new clothes. And *then* I shall see the sea for the first time.'

'For the first time? Well! Might tag along with you. Got nothing better to do. Tell you what, you look after that footman of yours and I'll go and get him some clothes. No, no. My pleasure. If I feel it all comes to too much, I'll let you foot the bill. Why, there's our Miss Trenton.'

Miss Trenton came into the coffee room and stood irresolute, her face a little pink and her eyes averted. But choleric as he was, the American seemed incapable of sustaining any animosity towards even such as Miss Trenton. 'Over here,' he called. 'We're making plans for the day.'

As Miss Trenton came up to them, he said cheerfully, 'Miss Pym has never seen the sea, so as soon as we make sure that Benjamin is all right, we're going out. Care to come along?'

Miss Trenton sat down next to Hannah, her back ramrod-straight. 'I cannot,' she said quietly. 'I need to go to an old friend who runs a seminary and ask for employment. That is, if she will have me.'

There was a startled silence. Miss Trenton gave a thin smile. 'As you have both probably guessed, I do not own a private carriage. I am an unemployed governess.'

110

'Yes, we knew you didn't have a carriage,' said Mr Cato bluntly. A shaft of sunlight shone through the leaded windows of the coffee room. 'Going to be a grand day,' went on Mr Cato. And to Hannah's horror he turned to Miss Trenton and said, 'Come with us. Put off your interview another day. We all deserve a holiday, hey?'

Tears started to Miss Trenton's eyes. She felt after the evening before that she had known the bottomless depths of humiliation and could go no lower, but what she had to say, she felt, put her beyond the bounds of ordinary human friendship. 'I cannot stay,' she said, 'for I would not be able to pay another night here. If I do not get this position, I do not know what I will do.'

She drew out a handkerchief and began to cry in earnest. Hannah still could not like her, but Mr Cato seemed considerably moved. 'Come, madam, I will pay your shot,' he said. 'Dry your eyes and keep Miss Pym company while I get some duds for our footman.'

Miss Pym and Miss Trenton were left alone. 'I suppose you despise me,' said Miss Trenton in a low voice.

'I despised you for your malice towards Miss Wilkins,' said Hannah. 'But for being poor? Nonsense. Wait here and I will see to Benjamin and we will have breakfast together.'

As she rose, the manager came up leading the physician, and Hannah took the doctor upstairs. He examined Benjamin's head and said he should stay in bed quietly for the day, but that the wound was clean and there was no sign of fever. Hannah wrote all this down for Benjamin and then rang the bell and ordered a large breakfast for the footman. She then wrote on a piece of paper, 'Do you want anything?'

Benjamin wrote in reply, 'Books or newspapers?'

Hannah ordered the morning newspapers from the waiter who brought in the breakfast and then went back to the coffee room to have her own breakfast with Miss Trenton.

Mr Cato returned in triumph with a red plush livery, rather worn, underclothes, shirt, stockings, and a pair of buckled shoes. 'How kind of you!' exclaimed Hannah. 'But will these things fit? The shoes, for example?'

'Bound to.' Mr Cato looked them over. 'I have a good eye for size.'

'Then I shall take them up to him,' said Hannah. 'It is very good of you, Mr Cato, and so I shall tell him.'

'Don't be all day writing things down,' said Mr Cato with a grin. 'You've got to see the sea.'

When Hannah had gone, he said to Miss Trenton, 'Don't go messing your face up with more tears, ma'am. The sun is shining and we shall all have a pleasant day. Then you may go to that seminary tomorrow and try your luck. She's bound to take you, ain't she?'

'I do not know,' said Miss Trenton. 'Oh, I was so jealous of Miss Wilkins. I have taught so many girls such as she – pampered and spoilt with doting parents, never having to worry about where the next penny is coming from, never having to grovel.'

112

'That's the way of the world,' said Mr Cato, 'and a nasty old world it becomes if you turn bitter, Miss Trenton, for people have a habit of giving back as good as they get. You cannot go around lying about carriages and puffing yourself up and sneering at people and expecting them to deal kindly with you, now can you?'

But such as Miss Trenton cannot remain in a state of humility for long. She began to feel that she was ill done by, that she had really done nothing wrong, that Penelope Wilkins probably was a trollop, but the prospect of a whole day's holiday with her bills being paid at the inn by the generous Mr Cato was not to be thrown away lightly. So she bowed her head and looked suitably ashamed of herself and Mr Cato smiled on her indulgently and reflected there was good in everyone.

Lord Augustus decided, not for the first time in his life, that a title was a very useful thing to have. No inn-keeper was ever vulgar enough to press for settlement in advance and he was able to hire a light carriage and airily ask for the charge to be put on his bill. He had discovered by inquiring at the inn that his uncle lived right in the centre of the town, and when he found the house his first thought was that his uncle was surely in straitened circumstances to live in such a place. It was a tall, narrow, dark building wedged between a haberdasher's and a jeweller's premises. He rapped on the brass door-knocker and waited.

After some time, a pretty little housemaid answered

the door. She bobbed a curtsy and took his card and asked him in a shy whisper to wait in the hall.

The hall, reflected Lord Augustus, was more like a cupboard. It was a tiny place dominated by a large painting of a sailing ship in full rig on one wall. The floor was sanded and a narrow uncarpeted stair led to the rooms above.

After some time, the same little maid pattered lightly down the stairs with the instructions that my lord was to follow her to the 'crow's nest'.

'How very nautical,' murmured Lord Augustus as he made his way up the narrow staircase after her. 'Why the crow's nest, child?'

'Because it's at the top of the house, my lord,' said the housemaid. Lord Augustus toiled up the stairs and then stooped his head to enter a small room that was like a ship's cabin. His uncle did not appear to have changed much with the passing of the years. The admiral was a small, slight man with a thin, scholarly face. The room was decorated with souvenirs from the admiral's travels – hideous wooden masks, small idols, brassware, carved ivory elephants, all lying about in a glorious jumble. At the window stood a large brass telescope.

Lord Abernethy, the retired admiral, had the same deep-blue eyes as his nephew. He did not rise to greet Lord Augustus but regarded him shrewdly. 'And what brings you, nephew?'

Lord Augustus sat down opposite his uncle and sighed. He had been about to say that he had come to Portsmouth to visit the old boy out of the kindness of his heart, but somehow he now felt that lies, even polite ones, would not do; in fact, they might hurt. He wondered why it had never crossed his mind or the minds of any of his roistering friends that the relatives on whom they so assiduously preyed might only pay up because they were lonely.

'The fact is, sir,' he said, 'that I travelled to Portsmouth to ask you for money. I then decided not to do so. I discovered to my surprise that I wanted to see you just the same, so here I am.'

Lord Abernethy looked quite shocked. 'What has been happening to you, my lad?' he cried. 'Methodists got you? The only time anyone of my age sees anyone of your age is when he's being sponged on. I admire your honesty, and yet righteousness sits oddly on you. We never were a righteous family, Gus, and that's a fact. You wouldn't like to try to wheedle some blunt out of me to put me at ease?'

'I cannot, Uncle. I brought a conscience with me to Portsmouth in the shape of an angular spinster with a crooked nose who was, I believe, at one time an upper servant.'

A slow smile curved Lord Abernethy's long mouth. He poured two glasses of wine, settled back in his chair, and said, 'Begin at the beginning.'

And so Lord Augustus told him everything that had happened with the exception of kissing Penelope. He told the story well and in detail, giving thumbnail sketches of the passengers.

'Carsey,' said the admiral. 'Lady Carsey of Esher. Now let me see. Old Carsey, that's Sir Andrew

Carsey, died last year. Fell down the stairs and broke his neck. Drunk, so rumour had it.'

'I am convinced that Sir Andrew was probably pushed down the stairs by his loving wife and had brandy or something poured over his corpse,' said Lord Augustus. 'What a rapacious female.'

'All sounds possible to me,' said Lord Abernethy. 'What did the bitch plan to do with that footman? Leave him to rot to death?'

'I do not know. Miss Pym said that the butler expected the cellars to be free for inspection in two days' time. That might mean she intended to kill him, or perhaps turn him loose, having had revenge.'

'And this Penelope Wilkins. I know old Wilkins, of course. Bags of money. Give him a civil nod when I meet him, but nothing more, mark you. He still takes off his coat and works in one of his shops if trade is pressing. Aye, and is not above going on board ships at anchor to sell his wares.'

'What is up with that?' asked Lord Augustus.

'Nothing at all, boy. Backbone of England, people like Wilkins. I merely pointed out the obvious that one does not socialize with such people.'

'Quite. But I wonder what work is like, Uncle. Such an exhausting bore trying to fill in the day with nothing but amusement. Such an expensive bore, too. While I am pursued by duns and lightskirts and matchmaking mamas, Wilkins probably falls into a dreamless sleep at night after a hard day's work and owing no man a penny.'

'But that is what the merchant class is expected to

do,' pointed out Lord Abernethy crossly. 'I do not like the turn this conversation is taking, nephew. I will put it to you frankly. Wilkins is one of the best, and yes, we have all heard in Portsmouth of the ravishing daughter he guards so close, but there is a gleam in your eye I do not like. I urge you not to entertain any tender feelings towards this little bourgeoise.'

'I have already been warned off by Miss Pym,' said Lord Augustus with a reluctant laugh. 'She considers me not good enough.'

'Impertinent baggage!'

'And between you, you have quite made up my mind for me. I shall call on the Wilkinses as soon as possible.'

Lord Abernethy glared at him and then his anger vanished as quickly as it had come. 'Whom you call on is your affair,' he said. 'I have not seen you since you went into the army. Did the life not suit you?'

'I had several unfortunate experiences,' said Lord Augustus drily. 'I was in Flanders with the 33rd under Colonel Wellesley to join the Duke of York's famous Ten Thousand.'

Lord Abernethy began to sing,

'The Grand Old Duke of York,
He had ten thousand men,
He marched them up to the top of the hill,
And he marched them down again.'

'Yes, that campaign,' said Lord Augustus. 'It was a hell of freezing cold. Wellesley decided that the

French would never fight in such bitter conditions but would hole up for the winter, and instead, they came speeding down the frozen canals, defeated the Dutch, and drove all us exhausted redcoats into Hanover and a new hell of cold and wretchedness. But the failure of the campaign can really be laid at the doors of the army brokers, those rascally crimps who created a flood of new field officers. For a cheap sum of money, anyone could be an officer – criminals, decrepit old men, schoolboys, and even madmen.

'After that, I went to India.'

'Should have made your fortune there,' pointed out his uncle.

'Everyone tries to make a fortune out of India. Let me tell you, sir, it is not just Warren Hastings who is at fault. Rapacity cannot be laid at the door of one man. Every grade of the East India Company, from the clerks in Leadenhall Street in London to its military and civil servants out east; every rank in His Majesty's army; and the whole array of native Indian rulers down to freebooters scouring the villages – all expect to rape India and line their pockets, and so I found out. I arrived in Calcutta a month before the hot season. I have never taken part in such a hectic social life. Major-General John St Leger was there. All the notables had their "seats". The diarist William Hickey had what he called his "little chateau" at Chinsurah, complete with verandas and Doric pillars. We rose every morning early and then played trick-track, or backgammon, as it is called here, till three-thirty in the afternoon. Then we dressed and took dinner at four and then began to push the claret about. At a dinner given by the 33rd, twenty-two healths were drunk in large goblets, after which we were permitted to go on drinking out of glasses of a more moderate size. Then, at two in the morning, we reeled to our palanquins and were borne to our quarters. I was weary of it all, but determined to stick it out until I had fought in at least one successful battle.

'And so it happened, I was in the Battle of Tipoo. We sailed from Calcutta to Madras and the ship ran on to a reef, but we all managed through sheer strength to refloat her. Then the pox of a captain, Captain Frazier, supplied us all with contaminated water, so we all got the bloody flux and that epidemic of dysentery killed fifteen good men. So, as you know, we won at Tipoo and I did well from the prize money. I sold out and took the next ship for home and prepared to spend all my energies in enjoying myself until the money had gone, and so I did.'

'And what are your plans now?'

'I think I shall return to the inn and see if any of the stage-coach passengers are left. You see, sir, we had so many adventures that already I miss their company.'

'You may rack up here as long as you like,' said Lord Abernethy. 'Meanwhile, I'll get my hat and walk with you to the inn. I have a desire to see these people. But you will find your adventures have given you a pair of rose-tinted glasses and that they will seem but a very shabby lot now.'

* * *

119

One day back home and already I am dying of boredom, thought Penelope. She had been sitting by the window all morning, waiting for the sound of a carriage arriving. She tried not to think of Lord Augustus, but Miss Pym had promised to call and surely she would.

But the more she tried not to think of Lord Augustus, the more she did. She could see his face clearly in her mind's eye, his blue eyes and beautiful face and golden hair. She could almost feel the strength of his arms. She could still feel his lips, she could still taste his lips, and it all made her feel wretched when she thought that a simple kiss could do such damage to her senses and leave him unscathed.

By late afternoon no one had arrived. And then she heard the sound of carriage wheels and looked down from the window. But it was only her father arriving home.

She flew down to meet him. She was suddenly determined to visit the inn and see Miss Pym and the others. Her father would take her.

At first, Mr Wilkins appeared reluctant. On reflection, he had been shocked by Penelope's adventures and alarmed that his daughter should have been in such danger. But when Penelope said softly that she was sure Lord Augustus was still there, Mr Wilkins brightened perceptibly and said that, after all, it would only be civil of them to call.

Mrs Wilkins, sitting sewing in the drawing-room, heard them leave and wondered where they were going. Only rarely did her husband tell her anything.

6

I . . . chose my wife, as she did her wedding-gown, not for a fine glossy surface, but such qualities as would wear well.

Oliver Goldsmith

Hannah Pym stood with her hands clasped in Portsmouth harbour. The sun was shining brightly and a stiff wind was blowing. Through the forest of masts gleamed the sea, endless and blue, sparkling and dancing and shining. She heaved a great sigh of sheer gladness. And then into that gladness crept a little tinge of regret. It would have been wonderful if Sir George Clarence had been at her side at such a moment: Sir George, that producer of miracles like ices at Gunter's and promises of opera.

'Doesn't it make you think, Miss Pym,' said Mr Cato at her ear, 'that stage-coach travel is as nothing

121

compared to travelling the world by ship? Do you see the packets and frigates? A steady wind and a man can be in America in twenty-one days. Think on it!'

'I have not yet exhausted stage-coach travel,' said Hannah, 'but it is all very exciting. Can we go somewhere where I can stand on the shore?'

'I'll drive you,' said Mr Cato, leading the way back to the pony and gig he had hired. He drove Hannah and Miss Trenton a little way out of town and then down to a beach. Great curling glassy waves fell at Hannah's feet as she walked in a happy trance along the shore. She felt like running and shouting aloud, but instead she contented herself by gazing her fill at the heaving ocean.

'Allow me to have a word in private with Miss Pym, if you please, Miss Trenton,' said Mr Cato and then walked away to join Hannah.

Miss Trenton watched them go. Mr Cato, she thought jealously, was going to propose to that Miss Pym again. She was anxious not to offend Mr Cato in case that gentleman regretted his generous offer to pay her bill at the inn, but jealousy of Hannah made her move towards the couple to see if she could hear what they were saying. The wind carried their words faintly to Miss Trenton's ears.

'Changed your mind yet about marrying me?' Mr Cato was asking.

Hannah looked at the fiery-faced American with some amusement. 'Mr Cato, I am persuaded you do not really care a fig for me. You know nothing about me. Why on earth do you want to marry me?'

'Fact is,' replied Mr Cato, digging one square-toed shoe in the sand, 'I came to England for the express purpose of finding a wife. I am not in the way of meeting the ladies back home in Virginia. I'm a bit awkward around them and that's the truth. I thought I would go to London and find me a bride. But it was just as difficult there. Friends tried to help me and produced likely brides, but I'm dashed if I knew what to say to them. All I want is a sensible woman who doesn't scare me. We should suit very well, Miss Pym.'

'Are you trying to tell me,' demanded Hannah, feeling piqued, 'that almost any female would do?'

'That's about it,' said Mr Cato, picking up a stone and throwing it into the curving waves.

'Then let me give you a piece of advice,' said Hannah tartly. 'If you should be fortunate enough to meet some other female who you think might suit you before you board ship, then I suggest you try courting her first.' Hannah was very annoyed. She had dreamt a little about telling Sir George of Mr Cato's proposal of marriage, but now she did not think it at all flattering to herself to relate that a gentleman had proposed to her out of sheer desperation.

Miss Trenton had managed to hear most of what had been said. She walked a little away again, her heart beating hard. If anyone would do, why not Miss Abigail Trenton?

Hannah was pleased to find Miss Trenton relatively good company for the rest of the outing and began to think that Mr Cato had the right of it – there was good in anyone, if Miss Trenton was any example.

They returned to the inn to change for dinner. Benjamin was up and dressed and waiting in Hannah's bedchamber for her. There was a small pile of gold and silver on the table beside the bed, which Benjamin proudly pointed out. He was wearing his new livery, or rather, new to him, since Mr Cato had bought the garments at a second-hand clothes-shop. He had curled his hair and powdered it.

'What is this?' demanded Hannah, indicating the money and turning so that her footman could read her lips.

He took a pair of dice out of his pocket and tossed them lightly up and down by way of reply.

'This gambling will not do. It will not do at all,' said Hannah severely.

Benjamin stood there with a grin on his face, a face that Hannah thought was beginning to look too cheeky and intelligent for a servant to have. Benjamin took out a new notebook and a lead pencil and wrote, 'I cannot hand it back now.'

'Oh, very well,' said Hannah, dividing the money into two piles. 'You take half. Go on. I should be furious with you, but I must confess I am pleased to have something to defray our expenses here and it would be hypocritical of me to pretend otherwise. But the day will come, Benjamin, when you will lose heavily. All gamblers do, and then I shall have to bail you out. Now leave me and wait below while I change and dress. Are you sure you are well enough to be up?'

Benjamin nodded vigorously, swept Hannah a low bow and walked out.

Hannah, Miss Trenton, and Mr Cato ate their dinner in relative silence and then retired to the coffee room. Hannah sent Benjamin to get his own dinner and said she would not need him for the rest of the evening.

'We should call on Miss Wilkins tomorrow,' said Mr Cato. 'It still feels strange, it just being us three.'

'I really meant to call today.' Hannah looked slightly guilty. 'But the sea, you know, the beautiful sea drove all other thoughts out of my head.'

'I could hire a boat,' said Mr Cato suddenly. 'The weather looks set fair. How would you like to find yourself out on the water tomorrow, Miss Pym?'

Hannah clasped her hands. 'Oh, that would be wonderful. What kind of boat?'

'Oh, a rowing-boat, I think. Take both you ladies.'

Miss Trenton gave a little sniff and then that irritating cough of hers. 'I cannot go,' she said. 'I really must go to see my friend and ... and ... find out whether she will take me.'

'Another day as my guest.' Mr Cato rubbed his plump hands. 'Hey, Miss Pym? What say you?'

Hannah wanted to say she would rather not go with Miss Trenton and yet her heart was touched by the governess's plight.

She forced a smile. 'Do say you will come, Miss Trenton.'

'You are the best of men, Mr Cato.' Miss Trenton gazed into his eyes. 'I shall never forget your generosity.'

'Nonsense,' said Mr Cato. 'You are both doing me

a favour. I have never felt more at ease with the ladies in my life before.'

'Why! Here is Miss Wilkins and her father,' exclaimed Hannah.

'I thought you would call,' said Penelope, rushing up to them. 'I waited and waited.'

'We meant to call tomorrow,' said Hannah. 'Pray be seated, Mr Wilkins.' Just then, she saw Lord Augustus coming into the taproom, followed by a small elderly man. 'Now we are all together again,' cried Mr Cato.

Introductions were made all round. Mr Wilkins was beside himself with joy. He was in the company of not one, but two lords. Hannah looked at his shining face and wondered if he stopped to think he might be betraying his radical principles. But it was obvious Mr Wilkins only wanted the best for his daughter and took the arrival of Lord Abernethy as a sign that a proposal was in the offing.

Lord Augustus was finding it very hard not to stare at Penelope. She was wearing a soft gown of white crepe decorated with a thin thread of silver. A spangled gauze scarf was worn around her shoulders. Her curls fell from a little knot on the top of her head. He could see that his uncle was giving her admiring looks, although Lord Abernethy was still rather stiff and formal when he spoke to Mr Wilkins, as if warning the tradesman not to become too familiar.

Penelope talked animatedly to Miss Pym about how life seemed very flat and dull after all the fun they had had, but all the while she talked she sensed, rather than saw, Lord Augustus, for she could not bring herself to look directly at him.

Hannah then began to regale the company with her impressions of her first sight of the sea, ending up with, 'And Mr Cato is to hire a boat on the morrow and take me and Miss Trenton on the water.'

'Please, may I go too?' begged Penelope.

'Well, puss,' said her father, 'I do not know that I approve. What if a squall should blow up?'

'We shall only go a little way from the shore,' put in Mr Cato. 'No doubt Lord Augustus will come along to help me with the oars.'

'My nephew and I have other plans,' said Lord Abernethy.

Really, thought the retired admiral, as a circle of disappointed faces looked at him. They are just like children!

'I am sure Uncle can spare me for a few hours,' said Lord Augustus smoothly, his calm manner belying the fact he found the idea of being near Penelope in a rocking boat where he might have an opportunity to take her in his arms a delightful prospect.

'In that case,' said Mr Wilkins quickly, 'I can have no possible objection, now that I know his lordship is to be of the party.'

Hannah, sitting next to Lord Abernethy, noticed his frozen expression, and when the others had begun to talk about when and where they would meet, she said to him gently, 'You obviously do not approve of your nephew's friendship with the Wilkinses.'

'No, ma'am,' replied Lord Abernethy. 'How can I?'

'Meaning that she is a tradesman's daughter? But if Lord Augustus returns to London and to his old life, he will go on gambling and roistering and die young. Miss Wilkins is just the young lady to give him a much-needed sense of responsibility.'

'I could not expect such as you to understand.' Lord Abernethy took out his quizzing-glass and surveyed Hannah coldly.

'I understand the ways of the world very well,' snapped Hannah, a high spot of colour on both cheeks. 'But I also know that there have been many successful marriages between members of the Wilkinses' class and the aristocracy. Dear me, my lord, you force me to remind you that many members of the top ten thousand got their titles on the wrong side of the blanket!'

'Miss Pym!'

'That is the case and well you know it. A girl like Penelope would breed fine strong sons. Tcha! You put me out of patience.'

Lord Abernethy's face relaxed slightly and a thin smile curled his mouth.

'I am not going to become exercised over your remarks, ma'am. My nephew has a great deal of good sense and knows what is owing to his family name. He will not make a mésalliance.'

'Perhaps it would be a mésalliance.' Hannah looked down her crooked nose at the little admiral. 'Miss Wilkins may be much too good for him!'

'Does that time suit you, Miss Pym?' Hannah realized Mr Cato was asking her.

'I am sorry. What time?'

'We are hiring carriages and driving out to a little fishing village, Croombe, along the coast. We meet here at two in the afternoon.'

'Splendid!' cried Hannah.

And all looked delighted with the arrangements except Lord Abernethy.

In her private sitting-room at another inn on the other side of Portsmouth, Lady Carsey looked up impatiently as her nephew, a thin, weedy youth whose highly rouged face showed signs of early dissipation, walked into the room. 'Did you find any of them?' she asked.

Her nephew, Mr John Fotheringay, grinned and slumped into a chair opposite and dangled one leg over the arm. 'Yaas,' he drawled.

'Are you sure?'

'All of 'em, I would say,' said Mr Fotheringay. He ticked off on his fingers. 'Item one: Female with crooked nose and funny-coloured eyes, spinsterish, square shoulders. Item two: Lord Augustus. I know *him* by sight. Item three: Dumpy little man with a red face and red hair. Item four: Another spinster, pinched little face, hideous bonnet. Item five: The almost unbearably gorgeous, most delightful little ladybird I ever did see. No sign of that footman you was talking about. Two men; one appeared to be the father of the beauty and t'other some sort of relative of Lord Augustus. But harkee, the ones you want are going to some village near here, Croombe, to take a boat out tomorrow at two.'

129

'Why? Why are they going?'

'Stap me. How should I know? Seems that one who answers to the description of the fire-raising Miss Pym wants a trip on the ocean. Probably that.'

'Good.' Lady Carsey ferreted in a box on a table beside her for a sugarplum, popped it into her mouth, and chewed reflectively.

'I need someone to do the dirty work,' she said at last.

'Just cross my palm with some gold and I'll do it for you,' said Mr Fotheringay and then whooped with laughter.

'No, nothing must lead back to me. This town is full of smugglers, is it not?'

'Crawling with them. I doubt if there is a house or inn in this town which has an honest bottle of brandy or packet of tea. This damn war with France has made everything so expensive, it is a positive duty to have one's own personal smuggler.'

'I need some smugglers. Get them for me. They cannot come here. Arrange some discreet meeting-place. You will be well paid.'

'Take a good few hours. And what do I tell them? They'll want to know if it is a killing matter.'

'Accidental drowning is what I am after. The sad fact is that Lord Augustus can probably swim like a fish, but he can't rescue all of them. He'll go for the beauty. The Pym woman is the one I want drowned like a rat.'

Mr Fotheringay's swinging foot paused in mid-air. He examined his buckled shoe carefully and then said in a neutral voice, 'Have you ever thought, Auntie, that you could save yourself a great deal of time and trouble by leaving them all alone? And what if the Pym female does drown? Won't that return to plague your conscience in the dark watches of the night?'

'Do not be stupid, John. If I let her go unscathed, *that* is what will haunt my dreams.'

'Well, you do believe in long-range murder. What did you plan to do with that footman if they hadn't rescued him?'

'Keep him until he'd had enough of a fright and then turn him loose.'

'I do not believe that for one moment,' said her nephew, who was allowed all the licence of a sort of court jester. 'The fellow would have run to the nearest justice and reported you.'

She shrugged her white shoulders. 'I would have denied it and so would all my servants. Besides, he cannot talk. Off with you, and get some clever silent type of smugglers, not some drunks who will promise all tonight and forget what they have promised on the morrow.'

The only people who found it hard to find smugglers were the excisemen. Members of the public who wanted some duty-free brandy or lace, coffee or tea found it amazingly easy. Mr Fotheringay simply went downstairs and buttonholed a waiter, slipped him a crown, and said he was looking for a fairly large consignment of brandy, and then winked. The waiter told him to ask at an inn called the Green Tree, down near the harbour. Mr Fotheringay

131

repaired there, pushed upon the door and walked in. He was accustomed to frequenting low taverns and knew as soon as he had walked over the threshold that he was in the right place. He bluntly asked the sleazy individual who was serving in the tap where he might find someone who could supply him with French brandy. The man said nothing. Mr Fotheringay cheerfully handed him a sovereign, ordered a glass of rum and hot water, and retreated to a corner of the room to wait.

An hour and several rums later Mr Fotheringay felt a large presence looming over him. A huge man in rough clothes was standing there, studying him. He sat down opposite Mr Fotheringay and said in a low voice, 'How much brandy?'

'None at all,' replied Mr Fotheringay happily, but the smile died on his face as he felt the prick of a knife against the back of his neck and realized the large man's companion was standing behind him. 'I mean,' he went on rapidly, 'I have an offer for you which will mean you earning a great deal of money.'

'That's more like it,' said the large man. 'Let's do the pretty and introduce ourselves all round. This here, behind you, is Ben, and I'm Josiah.'

'How friendly,' said Mr Fotheringay with a nervous titter. 'You may call me John.'

'Right, John.' Josiah leaned close to him. 'Out with it.'

So Mr Fotheringay explained that they were to locate a party who would be taking a boat out from Croombe on the morrow and they were to capsize that boat. That was all they had to do.

'It ain't a killing matter, then,' said Josiah reflectively.

'It probably will be, considering how few people there are who can swim,' said Mr Fotheringay. 'I want you to meet the lady who wishes this done. She will pay you well but the terms are to be set by her. She cannot come to a low place like this and you cannot go to her home. Where can you meet her where you will be unobserved?'

Josiah scratched the stubble on his chin. 'There's a house in Sheep Street, hard by a gin-shop.'

'Number?'

'Ain't got no number. Right o' the gin-shop. Anyone stops her, she can say she's meeting Josiah. Got that?'

'She'll be there in an hour,' said Mr Fotheringay, suddenly relieved that his part in the proceedings was over. He turned and looked at Ben, who was cleaning his filthy fingernails with the point of a large knife, and then scuttled off.

To his annoyance, his aunt stated she had no intention of going to Sheep Street on her own and her nephew must accompany her if he wished to see any of her money. She then loaded a brace of pistols, handed one to Mr Fotheringay, and tucked the other inside a large muff.

'I don't see why you don't take one of those villainous servants of yours,' complained Mr Fotheringay. 'Old Biggs, for example, looks as if he could slit a throat and think nothing of it.'

'Biggs is a fool. I have decided it is safer to deal only with you and your villains, John. Lead on!'

The smugglers found it odd doing business with what appeared to be a lady of the quality, although she was so heavily veiled they could not make out much. But she was generous, very generous. They received a bag of gold and were told they would get the other half after they had done what they were being paid to do.

'That's that, I think,' said Lady Carsey as she and her nephew walked away from the dingy Sheep Street.

'I think they're the genuine article, Auntie. Does it not bother you that they might take your money and not turn up?'

'I have dealt with men like that before,' said Lady Carsey. 'It's easy pickings for them. They'll do it . . . and so good-bye, Miss Pym!'

Lord Augustus wondered if he had ever really felt so young in his life before. There was such a beautifully carefree air of holiday about the party that assembled at the inn. Mr Cato was to take Hannah and Miss Trenton, and Lord Augustus had hired a light chaise, and, to Mr Wilkins's overwhelming joy, offered to escort Penelope. Repressing an urge to follow the party, Mr Wilkins went back to his business. His lordship should have plenty of opportunities to propose, and the presence of Penelope's father might throw cold water on the budding romance.

Penelope was wearing a dark-blue nankeen coat with gold buttons and a white collar. On her curls was a broad-brimmed straw hat. Lord Augustus thought she looked enchanting. But Penelope was suddenly very shy of him and could not find anything to say.

'Beautiful day, is it not?' asked Lord Augustus.

'Yes,' said Penelope.

'I suppose you are used to the sea and boats?'

'No.'

'Can you swim?'

'No.'

Lord Augustus laughed. 'You are not very nautical, Miss Wilkins, but you *are* monosyllabic. Do try to say more than one word.'

'I prefer to admire the view.'

They were bowling along one of Portsmouth's filthier streets where barefoot urchins played in the kennel and slatternly women lounged in doorways smoking clay pipes.

'Marvellous, is it not?' drawled Lord Augustus.

'I cannot be chattering all the time,' said Penelope. She was becoming irritated with him, because her body was aching in a strange way and something happened to her breathing every time his arm brushed against her own.

'Then I shall chatter for us both,' said Lord Augustus. 'You have all reformed me. I am determined to do something with my life.'

'And what is that?' asked Penelope.

'Well, for one thing, we are still at war and I am an able-bodied man doing nothing about it.'

'Were you in the army?'

'Yes, my chuck. Flanders and India.'

'And you did not like it?'

135

'No, but Flanders was a disaster and India gruelling. But at least I was doing something. Think, child, if all the men in Britain were like me, we would be overrun by Napoleon's troops in no time at all. Despite my good intentions, I might borrow money from my uncle after all and buy myself a commission.'

So he did not plan marriage, thought Penelope dismally, and yet why should she expect him to? It was all her father's fault, thought Penelope a trifle illogically. Mr Wilkins should have stuck to his principles and not have put ideas about marrying lords into her head.

'But when did you suddenly decide to re-enlist?'

'It is your fault, Miss Wilkins. You and Miss Pym. Between you, you have contrived to make me feel utterly worthless.'

'But it is in the nature of your class to be utterly worthless.'

Lord Augustus grinned. 'Not all of us, my sweet Radical. Faith! It is a perfect day for Miss Pym's outing.'

They had left the town and were travelling along a road by the shore. There was not a cloud in the sky. A brisk breeze was blowing.

'How odd,' said Penelope. 'The sky is so blue and yet the water is black. Why is that?'

'A trick of the light? Who knows?'

Lord Abernethy rose late and went up to his crow's nest at the top of his house. Although a wealthy man, it suited him to live in the centre of the town rather than in splendid isolation in some estate in the country. He loved to watch the ships coming and going through his telescope. He did hope his nephew was not going to make a fool of himself over the Wilkinses' chit, but decided he could easily put a stop to it by talking some sense into Mr Wilkins's head.

After a light breakfast of dry toast and weak tea, he settled down at the window and turned the telescope on the harbour. The room was so high up that he could look down over the roofs of the other houses.

He studied the glaring blue of the sky, the blackness of the water, and then felt a sharp rheumatic pain in his hip. He got up and went to a barometer on the wall and tapped it. The needle was slipping towards 'Stormy'. He gave an exclamation under his breath. Those fools, land-lubbers all, would probably put to sea not knowing the weather was about to make an abrupt and horrible change.

He opened the door and called, 'Mary!' and his little housemaid came running lightly up the stairs. The admiral kept few servants and all of them were women.

'Run round to the livery stables and get me a carriage, Mary,' said Lord Abernethy. 'And be quick about it. A fast-travelling carriage and a good pair of fifteen-mile-an-hour tits, and damn the expense!'

Mr Cato, who had already travelled to Croombe that morning, had hired a rowing-boat, which was resting at the foot of the jetty steps. The owner of the boat, a gnarled little fisherman, was pacing up and down.

'Reckon you shouldn't go out,' he said, looking anxiously at the blue sky. 'Nasty weather coming.'

'We are only going out a little way,' said Mr Cato.

The owner was reluctant to cancel the hire and so lose the generous sum Mr Cato had paid him.

'I'd be quick about it then,' he said, capitulating. 'But don't go out to the open sea.'

The party of land-lubbers cheerfully walked down the jetty steps and arranged themselves in the bobbing boat, Miss Trenton and Miss Pym in the stern, Penelope and Lord Augustus in the bow, and Mr Cato in the middle at the oars. Benjamin had been given the day off.

Mr Cato pushed off with one oar and then sat down and began to row smoothly. Lord Augustus reflected that Mr Cato was a surprisingly powerful man.

'Done much of this?' he called.

'Only on nice calm rivers,' shouted Mr Cato, 'but it's all the same thing.'

Hannah was quite dizzy with excitement. The slapping of the waves against the boat, the salt wind in her face exalted her. She felt like the veriest mariner of England.

Penelope sat next to Lord Augustus, her thigh against his thigh, and fought with a tumult of emotions. It could not be love, she thought. Love was something sweet and spiritual.

'Are we not going a little too far out?' called Lord Augustus.

'Oh, further!' shouted Hannah, her eyes flashing green. 'What power Mr Cato has.'

'Oh, yes,' agreed Miss Trenton, fighting gamely with seasickness but determined not to be outdone by Hannah when it came to compliments. 'You must be made of iron, Mr Cato.'

Mr Cato had a slight uneasy feeling that their rapid progress out to the open sea might be caused by a current, but the ladies' compliments went right to his head and he rowed the harder.

Hannah looked up at the sky in surprise. One minute it had been bright blue, as blue as the eyes of Sir George Clarence and just as sparkling, and the next it was a milky colour that was rapidly becoming grey.

They shot out past the long arm of the harbour and into the open sea. Penelope screamed as a wave curled over the bow of the boat and soaked her to the skin.

'Better turn back,' shouted Lord Augustus as the boat began to crawl up one large wave and then plunge down into a black trough of swirling water below another.

Mr Cato tried to bring the boat about. Another wave crashed over the side of the boat this time and Miss Trenton let out a high thin wail of terror.

'I'm caught in a current,' said Mr Cato.

Lord Augustus crawled forward and took a seat next to Mr Cato. 'Give me an oar,' he said. 'Between us, we'll make it. Stop screaming, ladies, and bail.'

Penelope and Hannah found a couple of pannikins and bailed for all they were worth. Miss Trenton sat in the stern praying loudly.

'We'll row to the left first,' said Lord Augustus to Mr Cato, 'and keep rowing until we get out of the grip of this current.'

Both men rowed as hard as they could while the waves crashed and tumbled into the boat and even the redoubtable Miss Pym was turning quite white.

'Now!' shouted Lord Augustus. 'Pull for the shore.'

They rowed hard, the going easier now. 'We're well away from the harbour,' said Lord Augustus. 'We make for the shore.'

'Thank God!' cried Hannah suddenly. 'Someone is coming to our aid.' Mr Cato and Lord Augustus rested on the oars and looked. A large rowing-boat with two powerful men in it was speeding straight towards them. 'Keep bailing,' ordered Mr Cato. 'It might be safer to let them take us on board. They've got a bigger boat.'

On and on came the other boat, at times almost hidden by the mounting waves, and then it appeared to come hurtling down on them from the crest of a high black wave and rammed them amidships with a sickening thwack. With amazing dexterity considering the height of the sea that was running, the two men turned their boat and headed for the shore. Not once had they even looked at the people in the boat they had just holed.

Water was pouring in. Hannah's life swirled before her eyes, eyes as full of salt as the ocean. All those years of service and a brief few months of happiness to end in a watery grave. She would never see Sir George again.

She could not swim. The water roared in her ears. She struggled up and her head broke the surface and then down she went again. She fought her way back up. One more look at daylight. Just one more look. And then as she was going down again, hearing a sort of confused shouting, something dug into her back and she felt herself being lifted up through the water. She blinked and found herself staring at the wooden side of a boat. 'Here's another,' shouted a voice. The grappling-iron that was dug into the back of Hannah's pelisse ripped the thin fabric and she felt herself sinking again and then strong arms seized her. She barked her shins as she was unceremoniously dragged on board and lay in the bottom of the boat, cold and shivering but miraculously alive.

'Sit up, ma'am,' ordered a familiar voice, 'and drink this.'

Hannah sat up and found herself looking into the face of Lord Abernethy. He held a flask of brandy to her lips. Hannah pushed it away. 'The others,' she croaked. 'What of the others?'

'Why, look about you!'

Hannah looked wildly around. She was in a longboat. Six burly rowers were manning the oars. In the stem was Penelope, white and limp, being cradled in Lord Augustus's arms. Beside them, Mr Cato was holding Miss Trenton, who was still crying noisily.

Helped by Lord Abernethy, Hannah struggled to join them.

She wanted to ask all sorts of questions, but she felt too tired and ill to manage to say anything. She turned her head away and was suddenly and violently sick over the side, getting rid of a great deal of sea water.

There was a reception committee waiting for them at the harbour: the local inn-keeper and two maids with blankets to wrap them in, local fishermen to support their faltering footsteps along the quay.

Penelope had recovered consciousness, although she was still being carried by Lord Augustus. Once inside the inn, Lord Abernethy ordered Lord Augustus to carry Penelope up to one of the bed-chambers and Hannah to accompany them.

Tears kept pouring down Hannah's face. She was so glad to be alive. How brightly the fire crackled on the hearth and how sweet to hear the rising storm raging outside the snug inn. 'Stay beside the fire,' ordered Lord Abernethy. 'I have sent to the George in Portsmouth, and to Mr Wilkins as well, for dry clothes for you all.'

Lord Augustus placed Penelope in a chair beside the fire and smoothed the wet hair from her forehead. He suddenly wanted to kiss her but could not because of his watching uncle and Miss Pym.

When the two men had left, Penelope and Hannah stripped off their wet clothes, dried themselves thoroughly, and then, wrapped in blankets, sat by the fire.

'How were you rescued?' asked Hannah.

'Lord Augustus. He can swim. He supported me as best he could. I owe him my life.'

'Thank goodness that uncle of his came just at the right time,' said Hannah. 'Oh, dear Miss Wilkins, I was so sure I was about to die.'

'But those terrible men. Why did they not see us? And having holed us, why did they not stay to help?'

'I do not want to alarm you, Miss Wilkins, but I am convinced they came out with the express purpose of trying to drown us. That was no accident. They were able to handle that heavy boat of theirs with ease. Could any of the others swim?'

'Mr Cato could not and he is such a heavy man that they had great difficulty in rescuing him, or so said Lord Abernethy, particularly as he thought the rescuers were those men who sank us and tried to fight them. But Miss Trenton could. I heard Lord Abernethy say she came swimming alongside, just like a cod in a bonnet.'

Hannah giggled.

Penelope began to laugh as well. Then her face grew serious. 'We must all get together and try to find out who it was who would wish to harm us.'

'The only person I can think of is Lady Carsey.'

'But she is in Esher!'

'She can travel to Portsmouth just as we did.'

'But would she risk doing such a thing?'

'Why not?' Hannah sniffed. 'All she has to do is get some of those villainous servants of hers to do it for her, although I did not recognize either of the men in the boat. The brief glimpse I had of them, they looked like smugglers. That is, they looked like fishermen, and villainous-looking fishermen are, I believe, always smugglers.'

'But how could Lady Carsey find smugglers? You cannot go out in the streets of Portsmouth and say, "I want to hire two smugglers."'

'In these years of shortage caused by that wicked French blockade, a surprising number of people, even in London, deal with the smugglers, and do not for one moment consider they are being unpatriotic in doing so. On the contrary, most Englishmen consider it their patriotic right to cheat the taxman. So all people such as Lady Carsey have to do is to put it about that tea or brandy is wanted and that way the smugglers are found.'

Penelope wrinkled her nose. 'But if it is so simple, why are so few of them caught? I mean, could not the excisemen simply pose as customers?'

'One brave excisemen did so. He testified in court against them. The following day his wife and children were murdered. They exact a terrible revenge. Everyone turns a blind eye to smuggling. What is the harm in a few bottles of brandy? That is how they look at it. And then few deal with them direct. The inn-keepers and wine merchants and grocers often buy from the smugglers; often, I gather from what I have read, are *forced* to buy from the smugglers. If Lady Carsey is at the back of this, then I do not think she quite knows what a hornets' nest she will have stirred up.'

They fell silent and then gradually both of them, overcome with fatigue, fell asleep, to be roused an hour later with the arrival of an anxious Benjamin bearing their trunks.

Briefly Hannah told him what had happened, forcing herself to form each word clearly so that he could read her lips, for she was too tired to write it all

144

down. She then dismissed the footman and she and Penelope dressed and went downstairs.

Mr John Fotheringay lounged at his ease in the coffee room at the George and waited for the news of any drownings. He did not want to ask outright and so draw attention to himself. He looked at his watch and then tucked it back into his waistcoat pocket. Nine o'clock in the evening, a raging storm blowing outside, and not a sign of the stage-coach passengers. Things were looking hopeful. So hopeful that he began to dream that the smugglers had been drowned as well. He had felt uneasy about using them.

The minutes ticked slowly by. People came and went. He shifted uneasily. His aunt could not possibly expect him to remain there all night. He decided he would need to ask some questions after all.

And then a party of young men came in, shouting for the manager and demanding rooms. The manager hurried up. 'We're all fully booked, sirs,' he said. 'Or that is, I think we are.'

'Think you are?' demanded the leader of the party. 'Speak up, fellow. You either know if you have rooms or not.'

'Fact is,' said the manager, 'several of the guests took a boat out in the storm along the coast and their luggage was sent for, but one of my waiters told me he had heard they had all been drowned. But I cannot give up their rooms to anyone else until I hear for sure.'

It was not a confirmation of drowning, but the weary Mr Fotheringay decided gladly that it was. He made his way back to Lady Carsey and told her cheerfully that all had been killed. She appeared neither glad nor relieved, merely indifferent. 'Here is the rest of the gold. You had better go and pay off the smugglers,' she said, holding out a bag.

'Do I have to?' said Mr Fotheringay uneasily. 'You are coming with me, ain't you?'

'Not I. This town wearies me. I shall leave for Esher tomorrow.'

Sulkily, Mr Fotheringay took the gold and, wrapping his cloak tightly about him, he headed out into the rain-swept streets of Portsmouth. He lost his way several times in the dark and was soaked to the skin by the time he found Sheep Street. He shivered as he knocked at the door of the building he had visited the night before. No one answered. He went into the gin-shop next door and asked for Josiah. He received first a blank look and then was told to be on his way. There were several evil-looking men in the shop, standing and listening.

'Two men,' said Mr Fotheringay desperately. 'Josiah and Ben. The house to the right.'

A thin man with a pock-marked face walked up to him. 'See here,' he said. 'There's no one there and never 'as been, so 'op it.'

Mr Fotheringay left and stood outside in the driving rain wondering what to do. The bag of gold was heavy in his pocket. Then he began to feel more cheerful. If the smugglers had wanted their money, they would have been there. Therefore, they must either have been drowned as well or decided to have nothing more to do with the matter. As far as his aunt was concerned, the gold had been paid over. He would keep it himself and take himself off to London, just in case she found out he had double-crossed her.

The smugglers had watched the rescue of the party from the shore. Both were uneasy. They never credited the rescuers with knowing about the storm that was blowing up but decided someone must have informed on them, and so they decided to lie low. They would stay away from their lodgings for that night, or at least until they were sure they were safe. If the mysterious woman who had employed them wanted them to try again, she could seek them out.

An hour after Mr Fotheringay had left the inn, the nearly-drowned party arrived, accompanied by Mr Wilkins. Upon receiving Lord Abernethy's message, he had come to Croombe to collect his daughter. But Penelope had insisted on returning with the others to the George. Someone, she said firmly, had tried to kill them, and they all had not yet had a chance to discuss it.

'Are you sure it was not just a pair of fools, playing a shabby trick?' asked Hannah. 'I thought at first that Lady Carsey might have found out where we were and sent someone after us. But now that I am warm and recovered, it seems too Gothic a notion.'

'Not entirely,' said Lord Abernethy. 'I caught a glimpse of them just before you went down. They looked to me like smugglers. No fishermen would be so callous. Have any of you had any dealings with smugglers?'

'How could we?' demanded Hannah impatiently. 'We have all but lately arrived in Portsmouth.'

'And someone must have overheard our plans,' pointed out Mr Cato. 'Someone knew exactly when we were sailing and from where. Did any of you note anyone paying particular attention to us?'

'I noticed a young fop in the corner who looked vaguely familiar,' said Lord Augustus. 'He kept looking at us but I assumed he was smitten by the fair Miss Wilkins.'

'So many people were coming and going,' said Miss Trenton. 'I should be frightened out of my wits if Mr Cato were not here to protect me.'

Mr Cato beamed and patted her hand.

'It is getting late and the ladies should be in bed,' said Lord Abernethy, getting to his feet. 'Coming, nephew?'

'I shall stay another night here, Uncle, and join you in the morning,' said Lord Augustus. He raised Penelope's hand to his lips and kissed it. Then he turned to Mr Wilkins. 'I would be honoured, sir, if you would allow me to call on your daughter at, say, four o'clock tomorrow?'

'Delighted,' said Mr Wilkins. Penelope blushed.

Lord Abernethy bowed to all and took his leave. Things were getting serious between his nephew and Miss Wilkins. He would call on Mr Wilkins himself in the morning and see what he could do to ruin the budding romance.

7

My affection hath an unknown bottom, like the
Bay of Portugal.

William Shakespeare

Mr Wilkins had a busy morning telling friends and
acquaintances all over Portsmouth that his daughter was
about to become wed to Lord Augustus. He even
remembered to tell his wife. Then he decided to go to
one of his shops and check the stock, always mindful that
he had a business to run, however exalted the company
his daughter proposed marrying into might be.

He was wearing an apron and in his shirt-sleeves
and balanced precariously on top of a ladder when he
heard a slight cough below him and looked down. He
turned a shade red with embarrassment when he saw
Lord Abernethy.

Mr Wilkins scrambled down the ladder and said with false joviality, 'You have caught me at my labours, my lord. What can I do for you?'

'Put on your coat and come with me to the nearest inn. I wish to talk to you,' said Lord Abernethy.

Mr Wilkins beamed with delight. He would need to get used to being on familiar terms with lords and ladies, he thought happily. He took off his apron and hitched his coat down from a nail behind the shop door and put it on, and then crammed an old-fashioned three-cornered hat on his head.

'The Feathers is hard by,' said Lord Abernethy, and without waiting to see if that hostelry suited Mr Wilkins, he walked before him out of the shop at a brisk pace so that Mr Wilkins had to scramble to keep up with him.

They arrived in the coffee room of the Feathers, where Lord Abernethy ordered coffee for both, not asking Mr Wilkins whether such a beverage was to his taste.

'Now, Mr Wilkins,' said Lord Abernethy. 'I will come straight to the point. I have always regarded you as a good sort of fellow in your way. But the sad fact is, I fear my nephew may be stupid enough to propose to your daughter.'

Mr Wilkins stared at him. He decided Lord Abernethy must be indulging in a little spot of banter and gave a dutiful laugh and then said, 'I am sure you have the right of it, my lord. But don't go calling Lord Augustus stupid. He is a fine young man and a credit to your family.'

Lord Abernethy picked up his coffee spoon and looked at it as though for inspiration. 'It will not do,' he said at last. 'You appear to have forgot, Mr Wilkins, your daughter's station in life compared to that of my nephew. Such as we do not marry into families such as yours. Miss Wilkins would be like a fish out of water. She would be much happier marrying one of her own kind.'

Mr Wilkins could hardly believe his ears. Having never before been on social terms with any of the aristocracy, and having become ambitious for his daughter, he had gradually come around to thinking that members of the quality were just like Tom, Dick, or Harry when you got to know them. He looked up and caught the slightly supercilious, slightly patronizing look on Lord Abernethy's face.

All his fury at a social system that put one above the other because of birth and lineage instead of hard work came rushing back.

'You have the right of it,' he shouted, getting to his feet. 'Demme, Penelope's too good for your nephew. She comes of good hard-working stock. Why should she throw herself away on a penniless Fribble who can't do anything at all? Yes, I know he ain't got a feather to fly with, for I checked up. A pox on you and your kind. Bad cess to you. You may tell that nephew of yours he needn't bother calling. He won't be admitted.'

Mr Wilkins stormed out, overturning his chair in his fury.

Lord Abernethy raised one long white finger as a signal to the waiter to lift the chair from the floor.

Then he leaned back in his own chair and sipped his coffee with enjoyment. Wilkins had reacted just the way he had known he would.

Hannah, Mr Cato, and, to Hannah's irritation, Miss Trenton, who, it appeared, was still Mr Cato's pensioner, called on Penelope at one o'clock, Hannah saying they should get their call over early so as to leave the field clear for Lord Augustus later in the afternoon.

'I think your Lord Augustus may have a proposal of marriage in mind,' said Hannah to Penelope.

'I fear not,' said Penelope. 'I have just been telling Mama that he plans to re-enlist in the army.'

Miss Trenton emitted a little laugh from the depths of another coal-scuttle bonnet. 'You are a romantic, Miss Pym. Lord Augustus surely never at any time had any ideas of marriage.'

Mrs Wilkins, a faded, crushed-looking, dumpy little lady who was sitting quietly netting a purse, spoke for the first time. 'Why?' she asked.

'Steady,' admonished Mr Cato in a whisper.

But to Miss Trenton, Penelope represented all the spoilt misses who had plagued her teaching life. 'Well, I mean,' she said with a titter, 'you can hardly expect an aristocrat to want to marry into such a . . .'

Her voice trailed away before the sheer fury in Hannah's eyes.

'What does she mean?' asked Mrs Wilkins.

'She don't know what she means, ma'am, and that's a fact,' said Mr Cato. 'She ain't nothing but a poor unemployed governess who rambles on.'

Miss Trenton saw all hopes of marriage floating away. She did not pause to think it was her own fault but only that life was desperately unfair. Her brief bout of humility at the inn had fled. She began to cry, 'Yow! Yow! Yow!'

'I see,' said Mrs Wilkins. 'Miss Trenton's almost rude remark was motivated by spite. Is that what you mean, Mr Cato?'

'Something like that,' said Mr Cato, as the yowling became subdued sniffles. 'We don't pay her any heed, ma'am. She's always coming out with nasty things. It's these hats of hers that make it all so odd, as if the coal-scuttle had upped and become malicious.'

'In any case,' said Hannah, who felt that Miss Trenton had borne enough, 'what are your feelings on the matter, Miss Wilkins?'

'I think everyone is rushing along too fast,' said Penelope. 'Papa could talk of nothing else but my forthcoming marriage. I think Lord Augustus likes me as much as any of you. Pray talk of something else.'

Mr Cato and Hannah began to tell Mrs Wilkins in detail about their adventures, Hannah correctly guessing her husband had told her very little. Mrs Wilkins seemed to enjoy it all.

The three visitors finally took their leave and Penelope rushed to her bedroom to put on a new gown of celestial-blue muslin which she could not help hoping would dazzle Lord Augustus.

She was seated in the drawing-room with her mother when her father erupted into the room and stood glaring at her. 'I have just given the servants

153

instructions that Lord Augustus is not to be admitted to this house,' he raged.

'Why, what has he done?' asked Penelope.

'He considers himself too high and mighty for the likes of us, and so that uncle of his told me.'

'But Lord Augustus did not tell you so himself?' put in Mrs Wilkins.

Mr Wilkins looked momentarily startled, not being used to much else from his wife but a sort of companionable silence. He stared at her and then stood, opening and shutting his mouth. Then he said, 'Yes, it was Lord Augustus who told me,' becoming even more angry at the distress on his daughter's face, distress caused by the whopping lie he had just told. 'He was there with his uncle and he laughed at your presumption, my girl.'

'It is all your fault,' said Penelope, getting to her feet. 'I would never have encouraged him, never even have thought of him, had you not gone out of your way to puff me up. Damn him, Papa, and damn you!'

She rushed out of the room.

Mr Wilkins stomped up and down in his agitation. To his surprise, his wife spoke again. 'When you are lying, Mr Wilkins,' she said, 'you always look straight at the person you are lying to, without blinking an eyelid. A most odd thing. I have oft remarked on it.'

'Mrs Wilkins! Are you trying to tell me that I have just told our daughter a pack of lies?'

Mrs Wilkins calmly drew some silk threads out of her work-box. 'Not about the uncle, but about the nephew, yes.'

'How dare you, ma'am.'

'I wonder.' Mrs Wilkins picked up a sharp needle and carefully threaded it. 'I have been frightened of your choleric tempers for so long, but I will not stand by and see our daughter's happiness ruined through false pride.'

'What are you going to do about it, hey?' he shouted.

'I do not know,' said Mrs Wilkins sadly. 'I wish I did.'

Penelope finally dried her eyes, put on a severe grey wool dress that she felt suited her mood better than celestial blue and trailed downstairs again to the drawing-room.

Her mother looked up. 'Your father has gone,' she said.

'I feel so humiliated, so stupid, Mama,' said Penelope wretchedly.

'Do you care for this Lord Augustus?'

'How can I . . . now?'

'The way I see it,' said Mrs Wilkins carefully, 'is that Mr Wilkins lied to you. Oh no, not about Lord Abernethy, but about Lord Augustus. It is my belief that Lord Abernethy tried to put a stop to what he considered an unsuitable marriage for his nephew, and Mr Wilkins, in a passion of shame, told you that Lord Augustus had joined in the sneering.'

Penelope gave her mother a startled look. Never before had she heard that lady voice what might be construed as a criticism of her husband. Hope rose in her eyes and then died. She sat down wearily. 'It is of no use, Mama. Even supposing, just supposing, that Lord Augustus wanted me, I would have to marry into a family that thought I was as common as dirt. In any case, this is all so silly. Lord Augustus himself has said nothing about wanting to marry me.'

'Nonetheless, this Lord Augustus saved your life. Not only your life but the life of that unfortunate footman. Such are not the actions of a dilettante. How sad if you let one retired admiral come between you without some sort of a fight.'

'Then shall we admit Lord Augustus when he calls?'

Mrs Wilkins shook her head. 'Mr Wilkins rules the servants in this household. They would not disobey him. I am not a courageous or resourceful woman, Penelope. But I think Miss Pym is. Why not get James to bring around the fly and drive you to the George? You will feel better if you talk it all over with Miss Pym.'

Penelope flew to her mother and kissed her. 'I will do that. Better to go somewhere than have the agony of sitting here, hearing him turned away. But if Papa has not been lying, then Lord Augustus will not call anyway.'

'Your papa was most definitely lying, child.'

Hannah, Mr Cato, and Miss Trenton were at dinner. Miss Trenton was inclined to be lachrymose, Mr Cato having said nothing about her staying on at the inn another day. Somewhere at the back of her mind was the growth of a niggling thought that she had brought it on herself.

156

All looked up in surprise as Penelope came in and sat down and joined them.

'What is this?' asked Hannah, looking at the clock on the wall. 'You should be at home awaiting Lord Augustus.'

Penelope dismally told them what had happened.

'I knew it!' said Hannah. 'I knew that old stick was out to spoil things. Your mama has the right of it, Miss Wilkins.'

'But what am I to do?'

'Let me think,' said Hannah.

Miss Trenton opened her mouth and then shut it quickly as Mr Cato glared at her. The fact that Mr Cato had obviously expected her to say something spiteful made Miss Trenton feel quite lost and tearful.

'Let us all take the air,' said Hannah at last. 'A little walk down to the harbour to clear our brains.'

Soon they were all walking through the narrow dirty cobbled streets that led to Portsmouth Harbour. The storm had fled, leaving the sky calm and grey, and a thin mist hung in the masts and shrouds of the great ships riding at anchor.

They were all standing in a group when Lady Carsey rounded a corner and saw them. She had been to the smugglers' address and had found them at home. They had told her that her nephew must have tricked her, and refused to hand back the gold she had already paid them, pointing out they had tried to do what she had ordered. Lady Carsey was clever enough to know she could not take revenge on these smugglers without bringing the whole angry hive of

157

them down about her ears. Her nephew she would deal with later. The sight of Hannah and the others, however, made her feel quite faint with anger.

She walked quickly and hurriedly away, the hood of her cloak drawn over her face. She would return to Esher, but one day, quite soon, she would seek out Hannah Pym and take her revenge.

Lord Augustus returned to his uncle's house after having been told by Mr Wilkins's servants that his presence was not welcome. This made him all the more determined to see Penelope somehow. But that determination soon died when he heard what his uncle had to say, his uncle being every bit as much of a liar as Mr Wilkins.

'I wish you had called here first,' said Lord Abernethy, 'for I had words with Wilkins this morning. The man is a Jacobin. Despises his betters. Said he did not want his daughter to marry a penniless waster. Said his daughter was a minx for leading you on, but that she had no intention of accepting your suit. Miss Penelope appears to think your courtship some sort of joke.'

'What is all this fiddle about my proposing marriage?' demanded Lord Augustus.

'They are very conscious of their wealth and of your poverty, nephew. You are classed in their eyes as an adventurer, about as welcome as a half-pay captain.'

'Damn their impertinence,' said Lord Augustus coldly. 'I'm going out for a walk.'

* * *

'The water is becoming so still,' marvelled Penelope. 'One would never think it had been boiling and raging only yesterday.' She leaned over the edge of the quay.

'Do not stand so close to the edge, Miss Wilkins,' admonished Miss Trenton. 'You might fall in.'

Hannah looked along the harbour and saw Lord Augustus and at the same moment he saw the group. His face hardened, his nose went up in the air. He started to walk forward and Hannah knew that Penelope was going to receive the cut direct.

Hannah was afterwards to wonder if there was not a streak of madness in her family. For she saw Lord Augustus and turned back and saw Penelope at the very edge of the quay looking down into the water, and the next moment, as if it had a life of its own, separate from her own body, Hannah's strong arm shot out and her hand landed squarely in the small of Penelope's back and she pushed her.

With a loud scream, Penelope toppled over into the water.

With an equally loud scream, Miss Trenton tore off her bonnet and, in front of Hannah's horrified eyes, jumped in after Penelope. There was a sort of moving blur beside Hannah and Mr Cato as Lord Augustus hurtled past and dived into the harbour after both of them.

'You pushed her!' shouted Mr Cato, dancing up and down. 'I saw you push her.'

'Something had to be done,' said Hannah sulkily. 'I had to bring them together. Why on earth does Miss Trenton have to play the heroine?'

'Because she's a brave woman,' howled Mr Cato.

Hannah and Mr Cato leaned over the edge. Lord Augustus had reached Penelope first. Miss Trenton saw him and turned away and began to swim neatly and efficiently to the nearest stone stairs that led down into the water.

'If no one else saw me push her,' said Hannah desperately to Mr Cato, 'do not, I beg of you, say anything. Please, Mr Cato, or you will ruin all.'

'I'll think about it, you madwoman,' growled Mr Cato, calming down now that he saw Lord Augustus had a firm hold of Penelope and was swimming with her to the steps which Miss Trenton was just beginning to climb. 'But if nothing comes of it, then I shall tell. You could have killed the girl.' He ran forward to assist Miss Trenton. A crowd was gathering. Hannah prayed Miss Trenton had not noticed that push. For if she said so, someone would call the police and the militia and she would find herself in a damp Portsmouth cell awaiting trial.

Fortunately for Hannah, Miss Trenton was basking in approval for the first time in her life. The little crowd sent up a ragged cheer as Mr Cato caught her in his arms, calling her noble and brave and courageous. Then came Lord Augustus, an arm around Penelope's waist, but his eyes still cold and angry. 'Everyone back to the inn,' he said. He hailed a passing hack and helped Penelope in and then climbed in himself, leaving Hannah, Mr Cato, and Miss Trenton standing in the harbour.

'What a silly thing to do,' said Lord Augustus.

Penelope let out a pathetic little sob.

He muttered something and gathered her to him. 'I could shake you,' he said. 'Why did you have to say that I was after your money and make a mock of me?'

'I did not!' cried Penelope. 'Papa told me that your uncle had jeered at him and said that your family would never stoop so low as to ally their name with mine. He said you jeered also.'

'How could I jeer when I did not even see your father?'

Penelope looked up at him. 'Mama said Papa was lying. That your uncle had probably said these things, but not you.'

He picked a piece of seaweed out of her hair. 'I think my uncle has been playing Machiavelli. Where did everyone come by this idea that I was going to propose?'

'I don't know,' mumbled Penelope. 'Stupid, is it not?'

'Yes, very stupid.' He looked down at her wet face and bedraggled hair. He gave a little sigh and gathered her closer in his arms and bent his mouth and kissed her, tasting salt water and salt tears.

Penelope struggled free. 'No, you shall not kiss me,' she said crossly. 'You are a rake and have kissed lots and lots of ladies. It means nothing to you.'

'It means all the world to me,' he said, suddenly happy. 'What a good idea marriage would be after all, Penelope. I could kiss you as much as I wanted, like this . . . and this.' He kissed her small nose, her forehead and the nape of her neck and then kissed her mouth again, this time with great passion, holding her so very tightly that her wet body seemed fused with his own.

The hackney carriage driver stood at the open door of the carriage and regarded the passionately entwined couple gloomily. 'The George, guv'ner,' he shouted hoarsely.

Lord Augustus dreamily freed his lips and searched in his pocket until he found a handful of wet change, the last of his money. He handed the lot to the gratified driver. He helped Penelope to alight and then, holding her hand, led her into the inn. 'I wish I had stopped to take off my boots,' he said. 'They feel as if they've got most of the sea in them.'

Lord Augustus told the inn manager to show Penelope up to Miss Pym's room. 'Do not go home,' he said softly. 'We must plan what to do. Stay at the inn until I return. Miss Pym will lend you some dry clothes. You will marry me, will you not?'

'Oh, yes,' said Penelope, her heart in her eyes. Oblivious of the watching guests, the dripping-wet lord pulled her back into his arms and kissed her soundly. Several cheered. Benjamin, who was silently watching, saw some men starting a book, laying wagers as to the length of the kiss, and cheerfully wrote down his bet.

That kiss went on and on until Penelope began to tremble with passion and Lord Augustus thought she was shivering with cold and instantly released her. 'Go along,' he said softly.

'One minute, fifty-nine seconds,' wrote down

Benjamin, who had been watching the clock. He handed over his paper and collected the winnings, having guessed the nearest time.

'Seemed more like ten,' growled one of the men. 'It beats me how they manage to breathe.'

Penelope sat by the fire in Hannah's room, but she had not removed her wet clothes. In all the transports of delight caused by the kisses of Lord Augustus, she had forgotten to tell him that she had not fallen, that she had been pushed, and she was sure it was Miss Pym who had pushed her. She had heard that spinster ladies often went mad in later years. She was not afraid of confronting Hannah. She knew she only had to scream for help to arrive.

The door of the bedchamber opened and Hannah Pym stood looking at her. Hannah saw immediately that Penelope knew it was she who had pushed her.

'What else was I to do?' demanded Hannah before Penelope could speak. 'That Lord Abernethy had told such lies, made such trouble. Then I saw Lord Augustus walking towards us and I knew he meant to cut us dead, and I . . . well, I . . .'

'Pushed me?'

'Yes, you see,' said Hannah, wringing her hands, 'I could not think what else to do to bring you together. And if it has not worked, then Mr Cato is going to tell the authorities, for he saw me, although Miss Trenton did not.'

'You deserve to be punished,' said Penelope, beginning to laugh. 'But, Miss Pym, it *did* work, and we are to be married and he is coming back here to

163

see me. Yes, I do forgive you, you terrible match-maker. Do give me some dry clothes.'

Hannah scrubbed tears from her eyes with the back of her hand, for she had been horrified at her own behaviour. Soon Penelope was dried and arrayed in one of Hannah's best scarlet merino-wool gowns and wrapped in a brightly coloured Norfolk shawl.

A waiter called to say that Lord Augustus had taken a private parlour for supper and requested their company.

Lord Augustus, after having given his uncle a blistering lecture, had found a jeweller open late and had sold a fine set of diamond buttons. He had settled his outstanding bill at the inn and started a new one by moving out of his uncle's and then had decided to entertain his old companions of the stage-coach. He had sent a note to Mr Wilkins's home, explaining his daughter was at the inn. Mr Wilkins was still working as he usually did. Mrs Wilkins received the note and prayed that the good sense of Miss Pym had worked a solution. After a few moments' hard thought, she amazed her servants by calling for the carriage and going off to the inn herself.

She found the party toasting the happy couple and listened in awe and amazement to the tale of the rescue. She hugged her happy daughter and gave her her blessing, but wondering all the time what on earth her husband was going to say. She drank several glasses of champagne and began for the first time in her life not to care a fig what her husband would say.

Hannah was elated, her odd eyes flashing as they looked around the table. But the travelling match-maker was soon to learn of a match that was none of her doing. Mr Cato got to his feet. 'A toast to *my* bride,' he said, 'Miss Trenton, God bless her. A brave woman.' There were cries of delight from all except Hannah, who felt rather sour. It was more than Miss Trenton deserved, a Miss Trenton who had found another hideous bonnet, albeit a small one, and whose nose was quite pink with gratification and relief and champagne.

And into all this merriment charged Mr Wilkins like a pantomime demon. He brushed aside all offers of champagne and seized Penelope by the arm and began to drag her from the room. Lord Augustus tried to pull him off.

And then faded Mrs Wilkins leaped to her feet with a howl. She knocked her husband's hat from his head, tore off his wig and jumped up and down on it, shouting, 'Selfish beast! I hate you!'

Mr Wilkins reeled back, releasing his daughter, who flew into Lord Augustus's arms.

'There!' cried Mrs Wilkins, kicking the mangled wig into the corner. 'There, you nasty, nasty man. Penelope *shall* marry Lord Augustus, and I have said so, so there!'

Mr Wilkins collapsed into a chair and clutched his shaven head. 'Has she run mad?' he asked feebly.

'We are simply trying to get you to listen,' said Hannah. Clearly and slowly, she told Mr Wilkins how Lord Abernethy had tried to split the couple apart, how Lord Augustus had once more saved Penelope's life. 'And look how happy she is,' said Hannah. 'Are you going to turn your own wife and daughter against you for life and all because of your silly pride?'

Mr Wilkins mumbled that he would agree to anything if only Mrs Wilkins would sit down and be calm. He looked every bit as frightened of his wife as she had once been frightened of him.

Everyone sat down again and a babble of voices tried to tell Mr Wilkins he was wrong until he clutched his head harder and begged them to stop.

'I don't like to be tricked, and that's a fact,' he said, 'and I believed everything Lord Abernethy told me.'

'The way to get your revenge on my uncle is by giving your permission to this marriage,' pointed out Lord Augustus.

'Perhaps, perhaps. But what have you to offer my daughter, my lord?'

'Not much,' he said cheerfully. 'An army officer's pay. I am going back to my old regiment and I am taking Penelope with me.'

Mr Wilkins was aghast. 'She has led a sheltered life. You cannot expose her to hardship.'

'I will cherish her,' said Lord Augustus. 'I will care for her, sir, and unless you want me to elope with your daughter, you must give permission.'

'Give it,' shouted Mrs Wilkins a trifle tipsily.

And so Mr Wilkins capitulated and the party resumed until Mrs Wilkins tried to stand on the table and sing and Mr Wilkins decided it was time to take her away.

Lord Augustus took Penelope home with her parents and then asked permission for a few moments alone with her.

He waited until he heard Mr and Mrs Wilkins walk up the stairs, Mrs Wilkins singing little drunken snatches of songs that no lady should know.

He smiled down into Penelope's eyes, took one of her hands in his, and sank down on one knee. 'I am asking you formally, Penelope, to be my bride.'

'Oh yes,' said Penelope, 'with all my heart. Thank goodness for Miss Pym.'

'What has our stage-coach spinster got to do with it?' asked Lord Augustus, getting to his feet.

'Do not tell, anyone, or she will be in the most fearful trouble,' said Penelope, beginning to laugh. 'But *she pushed me in*!'

'*What*!'

'Yes, she . . . she p-pushed me in the h-harbour b-because she was afraid you were going to c-cut me and she . . . she didn't know what else to do!'

'I'll wring her neck!'

'No, do not do that. She is the best of women. We have so little time this evening.'

Penelope stood on tiptoe and kissed him on the mouth, at first gently and then fiercely with all that pent-up burning frenzy of sweetness that she felt for him, until both were dizzy and gasping. 'We had better marry soon,' he said softly, 'although I do not think you can know what I mean.'

'I know what you mean,' said Penelope huskily. 'I am hungry for kisses. Kiss me again!'

8

These poor Might-Have-Beens,
These fatuous, ineffectual Yesterdays!

W.E. Henley

Hannah's departure from Portsmouth was delayed for two days. Lord Abernethy had originally reported to the authorities that 'two villains' had tried to drown his nephew and friends. Not much attention was paid to this. No one had died and the authorities decided that the said villains had been nothing more than a couple of youths messing about, who had not seen the other boat in the storm until it was too late. But when Lord Abernethy called to see how the investigation was progressing and demanded to know whether they had found the *smugglers*, that was another matter. The excisemen arrived on the scene and Hannah, and everyone else, was questioned over and over again.

In vain did Hannah suggest that Lady Carsey might be at the bottom of it. Wicked titled ladies were the stuff of novels. Smugglers were something else.

Hannah finally obtained permission to leave and booked two seats on the London coach for herself and Benjamin, Benjamin to travel outside this time like a proper servant.

On the evening before she was due to depart, Mr Cato and Miss Trenton were murmuring to each other in a corner of the coffee room while Hannah at another table regarded them with a jaundiced eye. Miss Trenton was being unbearably arch and flirtatious. Hannah did not think that lady deserved any happiness at all. She was relieved when both of them went out for a walk.

Hannah picked up a guidebook and tried to read it and then put it down with a sigh. She did not often mourn her spinster state, but the happiness of Lord Augustus and Penelope was almost tangible, and Miss Trenton was behaving like sweet sixteen. It was all very well to travel the roads of England as an independent lady, but what of the future, when her wanderings were over? She had a sudden bleak picture of a Miss Pym settled in some English village, damned as a nosy interfering woman as she tried to become involved in others' lives to relieve the tedium of her own.

A shadow fell across her and she looked up. Lord Abernethy was standing there. He drew out a chair and, without waiting for her permission, sat down opposite her.

He leaned back and surveyed her. 'I am glad to find you still here, Miss Pym,' he said. 'You see, I am persuaded that the engagement between my nephew and Miss Wilkins is all your doing.'

'They are very much in love,' said Hannah quietly.

'Love? Pah! What is love? Something that will soon wither and fade to leave two people washed up on the beach of reality, two people with nothing in common.'

'The fact that they have little in common may be the saving of your nephew's character.' Hannah ruffled the pages of her guidebook impatiently, as if seeking a chapter that dealt with recalcitrant uncles.

'I do not have such a low opinion of my nephew as you seem to have,' retorted Lord Abernethy sharply. 'I am most displeased with you. I would suggest to you that next time you consider interfering in the lives of others, you pause for thought. You will go back to London, happy to be the instigator of romance, and will not be around to see him tire of her and regret the day he became allied with such a low family. I detest stage-coaches. They allow the vulgar and common to travel the length and breadth of this land instead of staying in their own places of habitation and their own stations. Lord Augustus tells me he believes you were once some sort of upper servant.'

Hannah went very still. She felt the thin veneer of gentility she had acquired after her inheritance cracking and crumbling. And yet, Lord Augustus must have known that the reason she had a servant's gown in her luggage was not because she used it for fancy dress. Or perhaps Penelope had told him.

'I am a lady of private means,' she said stiffly. 'I see no reason why I should justify my ways to you. But I take leave to tell you, my lord, that you are a pompous and insufferably conceited man. Good evening!'

He rose to his feet. 'I feel our paths will cross again, Miss Pym,' he said coldly. 'And I have a score to settle.'

Hannah watched him leave. She found her hands were trembling and clasped them on her lap. Was she too presumptuous? Was she nothing more than a servant in sheep's clothing? she thought rather incoherently. What would happen when she went to the opera with Sir George Clarence? No matter how finely gowned she might be, would everyone see the servant beneath and pity Sir George for making a cake of himself?

She hardly ever felt tired, but she felt exhausted now. She miserably trailed up to bed, undressed, crawled between the sheets and fell down into a dream where she was at the opera and everyone was staring and tittering at her because she had not any clothes on at all.

Benjamin helped her on board the coach in the morning, before climbing on the roof. He kept shooting anxious little looks at his mistress, worried to see her so unusually downcast.

Hannah settled into a corner seat and looked bleakly out at the bustle in the yard. And then the door opened and Mr Cato and Miss Trenton stood there.

'We could not let you go without saying good-bye,' said the American. 'I have written down my address in Virginia.' He handed Hannah a piece of paper. 'Any time you get tired of Old England, write to me and I'll send you the ticket for a ship. Abigail and I will always be delighted to see you.'

Miss Trenton gave Hannah a thin smile.

'And when are you to be married?' asked Hannah.

'We'll be married on board ship by the captain,' said Mr Cato. 'Won't we, my sweeting?'

Miss Trenton tittered.

Hannah reflected she was glad she had had nothing to do with their romance. She would not be at all surprised if Mr Cato threw his new bride overboard before the ship reached America. 'We brought you something for the journey,' went on Mr Cato, handing her a box. 'Sugarplums.'

'How very kind.' Hannah cradled the box on her lap. 'I wish you both all the best. Why, here is Miss Wilkins and Lord Augustus!'

Penelope handed Hannah a flat box. 'From both of us, with all our love,' she said. 'Open it!'

Hannah opened up the box. Inside was a pretty little fan, small fans being the current fashion. It had tortoise-shell sticks and a dainty painting of a cavalier and his lady-love.

'How beautiful.' Hannah turned to the couple. 'Thank you both very much.' Other people began to board the coach. More were climbing on the roof.

'Going to be a crowded journey,' said Lord

Augustus. 'Do not fall into any more adventures, Miss Pym. I fear you have had enough.'

'Out of the way,' said the guard. 'We're moving off.' He slammed the door of the coach shut. Hannah let down the glass and leaned out of the window. 'Are you really happy, Miss Wilkins?' she asked Penelope.

Penelope stood on tiptoe and kissed Hannah's cheek. 'So very happy,' she said, her eyes shining.

Comforted, Hannah sat down in her seat as the guard blew a fanfare from the roof and the coach rumbled forward.

'Good-bye,' shouted the small group in the inn yard, waving their handkerchiefs, and Hannah waved back until the coach turned out into the street and she could see them no more.

Lord Augustus drove Penelope through the quiet morning streets of Portsmouth. 'I am amazed you got permission to come along to the inn with me to say good-bye to Miss Pym,' he said.

Penelope laughed. 'It was all Mama's doing. She told me to go and not to trouble Papa with it. He is quite nervous of her now. But he is reconciled to having you as a son-in-law and is back to bragging to his friends that his daughter is going to marry a lord.'

'My uncle is not reconciled at all,' said Lord Augustus with a rueful grimace.

'Shall I have the same trouble with your family?' asked Penelope nervously.

'I have not the faintest idea,' said Lord Augustus

candidly. 'But it really doesn't matter, Penelope. We shall not be living with them. I was not brought up like you. I went straight to the army after Eton. I do not think my parents ever had much to do with me from the day I was born. I was given to a wet-nurse, then a nurserymaid, and then a tutor and then school. I cannot say I know my parents at all well. I am not the heir, so they are usually content to leave me to my own devices.'

'And you will not ever be ashamed of me?' Penelope put a hand on his arm and looked up into his face.

He reined in his horses and turned to her. 'I shall always be proud of you,' he said. 'Kiss me, Penelope.'

And so she did. Their embrace was silent and passionate, their emotions holding them so still that a curious sea-gull perched on the carriage rail and watched them with unblinking eyes while a red sun rose over Portsmouth to herald another day.

Hannah felt comforted by the fact that everyone had come to see her off, and yet Lord Abernethy's words still burnt in her brain.

And so she was unaware of the impressed looks of the other passengers when she sat down to meals with a liveried footman at attention behind her chair. There was a pretty young miss on board and a thin clerk who looked at her with hungry eyes. Hannah barely noticed. The Hannah Pym of the down trip would promptly have turned her energies into

174

throwing them together. The Hannah Pym of the up trip was determined to mind her own business from now until the end of time.

But as the coach eventually rolled into London, Hannah's spirits began to lift. The very air of London seemed to permeate the carriage, a sort of strung-up excitement.

Then she thought of Benjamin. What was she to do with him?

When they alighted in Piccadilly, she hailed a hack and gave her address in Kensington. She turned to face Benjamin. 'You cannot stay with me,' she enunciated, forming the words slowly. 'We will leave our bags and then find a room for you and I will do my best to find you a position.'

Benjamin shook his head vigorously and looked stubborn. 'You will do as you are told,' said Hannah sharply, but Benjamin had turned his head away.

It was wonderful to see all the familiar sights, thought Hannah. There was Hyde Park Corner with Apsley House, residence of Lord Apsley, the Lord Chancellor, on one side, and the red brick front of St George's Hospital on the other.

Then the village of Knightsbridge with its scattered cottages and maypole on the village green. And then over the Knight's Bridge, a little stone bridge, and so along the muddy road to Kensington.

Benjamin paid the hack and lifted Hannah's trunks and a bag of his own. He appeared to have been shopping in Portsmouth. Hannah was amazed at the way Benjamin always seemed to get money from his gambling. She sometimes wondered if the dice he carried in his pocket were loaded.

She collected her key from the baker and mounted the stairs to her small apartment.

Benjamin looked around him and then frowned. He took out his notebook and wrote, 'This will not do for us.'

'It does very well for me,' retorted Hannah as he studied her lips to find out what she was saying. Benjamin shook his head so hard that a little snowstorm of powder drifted down on to the bare boards of the room. Then he bowed and stalked out.

Well, really, thought Hannah, half exasperated, half amused. I do believe my high and mighty Benjamin has taken me in dislike because of my humble surroundings. Ungrateful wretch!

She made herself some tea and sat down to drink it. Slowly her eyelids began to droop. She put down the cup and fell fast asleep.

She awoke two hours later to find Benjamin standing over her.

He held out a piece of paper on which he had written, 'Come. I have found a place for us.'

Hannah rubbed her eyes and read it again. Then she shook her head. Benjamin thrust another sheet of paper in front of her. On it he had written, 'A lady of Your Consekwence should not dwel in a Hovel!'

'Benjamin, you are a stubborn man,' said Hannah. But she was suddenly so delighted that he had come back that she decided to humour him.

She put on her hat and followed him out. He had a

hack waiting. 'Where are we going?' mouthed Hannah, but Benjamin would only grin.

The hack drove back to the West End of London and stopped finally in South Audley Street, off Grosvenor Square. Benjamin must have run mad if he thinks I can live here, thought Hannah, but she followed him from the hack. He produced a large key and opened the street door to a trim white stuccoed house and led the way to the first floor and, producing another key, opened that door and led Hannah inside.

It was a pretty little flat, tastefully furnished. It consisted of a sitting-room, a parlour, a small kitchen like a cupboard, a bedroom, and then a smaller, cell-like room that Benjamin indicated proudly would be his own.

It was clean and light and airy. Above all, it was a superbly fashionable address.

'How much?' demanded Hannah.

Benjamin wrote down, 'Eighty pounds a year.'

'Eighty pounds!' Hannah raised her hands in horror.

She was about to write down a firm NO, when she suddenly paused. She meant to retire to the country the following year. She could perhaps take it for a year. She would be very near Sir George Clarence. She could entertain in a very small way, a tea-party, for example. How could she expect to become a lady living over a bakery in the village of Kensington?

She looked at Benjamin and nodded reluctantly.

* * *

Hannah found she had fallen in love with her new abode. Here she was, right in the centre of fashionable London. She had written out her first cheque – one for the year's rent – slowly and with great trepidation. Benjamin was installed in his cell. He had found a bed, a table, and a chair. As usual, he refused to accept any money from Hannah, a Hannah who, still smarting from Lord Abernethy's remarks, complained crossly that her footman must stop treating her like a pauper. But then she suddenly became aware of the social advantage of having a footman. Benjamin could take a letter to Sir George Clarence and inform that gentleman of her return. Hannah wanted to remind him of his offer to take her to the opera, but did not dare.

Sir George Clarence was reading the newspapers when Benjamin arrived with Hannah's letter. He read it and then looked up in surprise as his servant told him that Miss Pym's footman was waiting in the hall in case there was any reply.

Sir George was at first startled and then assumed that Miss Pym had sent one of her own former colleagues to act as messenger. He remembered clearly having offered to take his brother's ex-housekeeper to the opera. He pulled forward a sheet of paper and then hesitated as he glanced at the address on Hannah's letter – a very fashionable address. She would not keep much of her legacy at this rate, he thought. To take the housekeeper to Gunter's was one thing, to appear with her at the opera was another. And yet he had promised, and he remembered the way those odd eyes of hers had glowed with delight.

He would call on her, he decided. No need to make his mind up right away.

Hannah broke the seal of his letter impatiently while Benjamin regarded his mistress bursting with curiosity.

'Thank you for going to Sir George Clarence,' said Hannah. 'Watch my mouth, Benjamin, and I will tell you how I came to meet him.'

She described her late employer, her legacy, and the kindness of Sir George. 'And he is coming here this afternoon, Benjamin! What shall I give him?'

Benjamin held up his hand and then pointed to his chest, indicating he would handle everything.

Sir George had said he would call at three. By half past two, Hannah was seated and dressed, and in an agony of anticipation. She was wearing a white muslin gown with a blue spot under a Turkish vest of black velvet. On her sandy hair was a Turkish turban made of blue muslin with a falling edge fringed in gold. She had a pair of the latest shoes on her elegant feet, thin slippers of blue kid, without heels. She began to speak aloud, practising her vowels. No one said 'obleege' any more; it was now oblige. No one said 'Lonnon' these days; all pronounced it London.

And then she heard a knock at the street door and Benjamin pattering lightly down the stairs to answer it, Benjamin who had appeared that morning in a new pair of thin leather pumps to replace the heavy shoes Mr Cato had bought him.

Sir George's first uneasy feeling was that Miss Pym had joined the ranks of the Fashionable Impure. First, there was the footman, not a colleague, but obviously Hannah's servant. Then there was the elegant flat. And then there was Miss Pym, a Miss Pym on whom the fashionable clothes sat well. Before, he reflected, she had looked as if she had only borrowed them for the day.

But the minute she began to speak, he knew that Miss Pym was as respectable as ever. She was so open, so frank, so obviously delighted to see him. The day was chilly and a fire blazed on the clean hearth. The footman came in and put down a plate of thin sandwiches and a plate of cakes and then proceeded to make a pot of tea in an elegant pot and pour it into delicate cups.

Hannah wondered uneasily how Benjamin had come by the china.

Sir George pressed Hannah to tell him of her latest adventures and then leaned back in his chair and listened in amazement to a tale of hanging, wrecked carriage, kidnapped footman, burnt house and near drowning.

'My dear Miss Pym,' he exclaimed at last, 'surely you have had your fill of adventures?'

'I thought I had,' said Hannah, thinking of her depression after Lord Abernethy's call. 'But I shall go on a little journey next time, perhaps to Brighton. Oh, to see the sea again, Sir George!'

Sir George looked at her with affection and decided on the spot that he would take her to the opera after all. She amused him as no other woman had ever done and he often found the days of his retirement long and wearisome.

'I have not forgotten my invitation to the opera,' he said. 'Would tomorrow night be too soon? I can call for you at eight.'

Hannah's odd eyes glowed. 'I would love to go,' she said, and then, as soon as the words were out of her mouth, she realized she had nothing to wear. Fortunately, Sir George immediately took his leave and did not notice that Hannah was becoming more depressed by the minute.

'Benjamin, what am I to do?' wailed Hannah. 'He has asked me to the opera and I have not a suitable gown. I took some of my late employer's wife's clothes – with permission, of course, but I did not imagine at the time that I would be going to places like the opera house.'

Benjamin looked at her, his head a little on one side, his eyes bright and intelligent.

'And where did you find the china, Benjamin?'

The footman wrote down, 'Borrowed.'

'From whom?' asked Hannah.

He wrote down, 'Butler in household near here.'

'I am surprised you know any servants at all,' said Hannah. 'For it is my belief that before Lady Carsey you had not worked in service.'

Benjamin looked hurt.

'No, it is not an insult,' said Hannah, 'and you are the best of fellows. But you must remember I am a servant myself, or was one until recently. The women are all very well, but footmen can be lazy and frivolous and not very bright.' Her thoughts flew to Mrs Clarence. The footman she had run off with had been very handsome and charming but certainly not very intelligent. Then her thoughts returned abruptly to her present problem and she sighed.

'I shall try to think of something, Benjamin, but I fear I am going to have to refuse Sir George's invitation.'

Benjamin went silently away and cleaned and packed the borrowed china and took it to the butler two doors away. He had gambled with the butler and then asked for the loan of good china in lieu of payment. The butler looked immensely relieved to get it back.

The footman stood in the butler's little pantry and slowly tossed the dice up and down. 'No, you don't,' said the butler. 'Once bitten . . .' A bell clanged from upstairs. 'That's my lord and lady,' exclaimed the butler. 'Going out.'

Benjamin waited in the pantry for a few moments and then went out of the servants' door and climbed the area steps. Lord and Lady French, the butler's employers, were getting into their carriage. Benjamin studied Lady French with interest. She was a thin, spare, middle-aged woman, very fashionably dressed.

He darted back down the stairs. The butler exclaimed with annoyance when he returned. 'It's no use hanging around here, fellow. I think them dice you got was loaded.'

Benjamin wrote down, 'Use any dice you like.'

The butler hesitated and then grinned. 'Got an hour to spare,' he said. 'But *my* dice, this time.'

After an hour in the servants' hall, the butler clutched his wig and moaned, 'I must ha' been mad. That's half a year's pay you've got off o' me.'

Benjamin smiled at him gently and wrote down, 'I need to borrow something else. Lend it to me and I'll forget your debt.'

Hannah awoke the next day wondering why she felt so low. Then she remembered. She would need to pluck up courage and tell Sir George she could not go to the opera.

She sat up in bed and then stared in surprise at what lay across the bottom of it.

She slowly got up and went and picked up the splendid opera gown that was lying there. It was of rich plum-coloured velvet ornamented with gold embroidery. Beside it lay an opera cloak of gold lamé.

She went into Benjamin's room and jerked her head as a signal that he was to follow her.

Benjamin, in his shirt-sleeves, breeches and bare feet, and yawning loudly, trailed after her.

Hannah pointed to the clothes. Benjamin disappeared and returned with a sheet of paper on which he had already written that he had managed to borrow the clothes but was sworn to secrecy as to where they came from and, no, he had not stolen them.

Hannah picked up the gown and held it against her. She somehow knew it would be a perfect fit. Her hand smoothed the beautiful material, and all in that moment, she decided she did not care how Benjamin had come by it. She would go to the opera.

The opera was a blaze of light and jewels. Hannah felt just as nervous as if she were about to go on stage. She felt Sir George was looking overwhelmingly grand in a silk coat of dark blue with diamond buttons, a fall of lace at his throat, and a dress-sword with a jewelled hilt at his hip. His white hair gleamed silver in the candlelight and his blue eyes were warm and merry.

Hannah was in such a state of rapture, combined with acute nervousness, that she thought she might faint. She sat down very gingerly on the edge of her chair and looked around her with dazed eyes.

The opera was an Italian one by Giovanni Pergolesi called *La Serva Padrona*, which Sir George explained meant 'The Maidservant Turned Mistress'.

Practically all of society went to the opera to see each other and to be seen. Sir George reflected it was a novelty to entertain a lady who had come to see what was on the stage. From the moment the curtain rose on the first act, Hannah was enchanted with the frothy plot of the maid-servant who tricks her master into marrying her. To her relief it was sung in English, so she could follow every word. Lord Abernethy's harsh words were a thing of the past. Hannah had recovered all her child-like capacity of treasuring the moment. The voices of the opera singers coiled round her heart. At the interval, she was so proud of being escorted by such a fine gentleman as Sir George that she felt her happiness was close to tears.

But her evening did not end with the opera. There was a ball afterwards. Hannah knew how to dance, as the servants at Thornton Hall, when Mrs Clarence had been in residence, had enjoyed almost as many dances in the servants' hall as their betters did abovestairs.

She danced a creditable minuet with Sir George and then sat at his side, where she enjoyed watching the other guests, too happy to be aware that speculative eyes were being cast in her direction and various dowagers were wondering sourly if that confirmed bachelor, Sir George, had fallen at last.

And then there was the carriage ride home in the small hours of the morning, the air of Covent Garden full of the smells of fruit and vegetables from the nurseries of Kensington as the market prepared for the morning's trade.

But nothing, nothing at all in that whole magical evening could match the moment when Sir George helped Hannah down from his carriage in South Audley Street and raised her hand to his lips.

Benjamin was waiting at the top of the stairs to take Hannah's cloak, to lead her to a seat by the fire, to lean forward and watch her lips as she poured out all the glories of the evening.

When she had at last fallen silent, Benjamin wrote down, 'When will you see him again?'

Hannah clasped her hands. She knew she could not bear to wait in London hoping he would call. If he did not call, then she felt her heart would break.

'After Brighton,' she said. 'We will go to Brighton, and *then* I shall see him again.'